NEWARK. OHIO 43055

W9-BOA-345

3 2487

WESTERN

D W

Large Print Ols
Olsen, Theodore V.
Eye of the wolf

WITHDRAWN

14 DAYS

NEWARK PUBLIC LIBRARY
NEWARK, OHIO

GAYLORD M

EYE OF THE WOLF

T. V. Olsen

Chivers Press • G.K. Hall & Co.
Bath, England   Thorndike, Maine USA

This Large Print edition is published by Chivers Press, England, and by G.K. Hall & Co., USA.

Published in 1998 in the U.K. by arrangement with Golden West Literary Agency.

Published in 1998 in the U.S. by arrangement with Golden West Literary Agency.

U.K. Hardcover ISBN 0–7540–3295–7 (Chivers Large Print)
U.K. Softcover   ISBN 0–7540–3296–5 (Camden Large Print)
U.S. Softcover   ISBN 0–7838–8457–5 (Nightingale Series Edition)

Copyright © 1971 by T.V. Olsen
Copyright © 1973 by T.V. Olsen in the British Commonwealth

All rights reserved.

All of the characters in this book are fictitious, and any resemblance to actual persons, living or dead, is purely coincidental.

The text of this Large Print edition is unabridged.
Other aspects of the book may vary from the original edition.

Set in 16 pt. New Times Roman.

Printed in Great Britain on acid-free paper.

British Library Cataloguing in Publication Data available

Library of Congress Cataloging-in-Publication Data

Olsen, Theodore V.
    Eye of the wolf / Theodore V. Olsen.
        p. (large print)   cm.
    ISBN 0-7838-8457-5 (lg. print : sc : alk. paper)
    1. Large type books.   I. Title.
    [PS3565.L8E9   1998]
    813'.54—dc21   98-10487

NEWARK PUBLIC LIBRARY
NEWARK, OHIO 43055-5087

CHAPTER ONE

He rode out of the dusty pines to the edge of the road and stopped. He hesitated. It was the same twinge of reluctance in him every time, coming down from his mountains to the clot of frame-and-'dobe buildings that made up the town called Spurlock. Sitting his paint horse under the trees, he had the unthinking grace of all horsemen—a slim whip of a youth in a faded blue-and-white-checked calico shirt worn with the tails out and wear-grayed Levi's whose soft fray clung to his long catty legs.

The paint was patient, trained, gaunt-barreled, an old partner of his master's. He sat utterly still except for twitching his tail at flies now and then. A leadrope trailed from the saddle pommel to a rope bridle on the rangy white colt following them. He was nearly three years old, his small head and sleek arch of neck pointing to strong Arabian blood, while the sinewy power of his legs and his deep chest showed the still-developing musculature of his mustang heritage. He swung his head, stamping restively.

The youth looked around. '*Ho-shuh*,' he said.

The colt fidgeted a little more, a spurt of defiance for the horse-calming word, then quieted.

Large Print Ols
Olsen, Theodore V.
Eye of the wolf

502 6969

The late sun of this May afternoon sprinkled fragile flakes of light through the needle-burred boughs, slanting a mild warmth into the youth's coffee-brown face. It was a thin face, fine-featured, rescued from delicacy by the pointed angles of jaw and cheekbones. His shoulder-length hair—black, thick, coarse as horsemane—was held back from his eyes by a strip of red worsted tied around his temples. Below it, his eyes were gray-dark, the color of fresh mortar. Young Will-Joe Cantrell, son of a Navajo woman who had hated the sight of him and a white man he had never seen, was eighteen this spring.

The colt stamped again. Will-Joe said, 'All right,' speaking English, his voice solemn and soft, faintly guttural with the swallowed word-ends of his Navajo upbringing.

He nudged the paint forward into the road, tugging the colt along, rocking easy to his mount's gait. Sun winked dully off the silver conches on the rawhide belt circling his waist over his shirt. In a land where half the grown men wore waist guns, his belt held only a knife in a beaded sheath, its hilt inset with silver and lapis lazuli. A Winchester rifle was snugged in the boot under his right knee.

He had dropped most of the way down along the peaks shouldering the north end of Spurlock Valley before hitting the road, but even close to the valley floor it still switchbacked like a chocolate snake. The spring mud had shriveled to a damp ochre clay that balled the paint's hoofs, making him fiddlefoot with discomfort.

Will-Joe's nose twitched. He could smell it already—the town. Still hidden from his sight, it sent mingled odors of stables, supper-hour smoke, cookery and other familiar yet unidentifiable white-man scents up along the stealthy wind currents. Will-Joe could hardly abide some of the smells that surrounded white men—few Indians could—but old Adakhai had always cautioned him on the fine points of courtesy when dealing with men whose ways were strange.

And the whites still seemed strange to Will-Joe although, he supposed, he was now living as much like a white man as like a Navajo. He used white man's gear and Indian methods to trap his horses. He sold his rough-broken stock to white buyers and used the money to buy his few wants at the Spurlock stores, going down maybe once in three months. As he never visited his mother's people, he rarely heard his Navajo name, Jahzini. Since he dealt mostly with whites now, he'd added his father's last name to the mission name of Will-Joe he'd been given as a boy. Saul Cantrell—he knew that about his father, the real or false name he'd gone by.

And that was almost all he knew.

The road made a crook up ahead. Nearing it, Will-Joe heard a wagon approaching, its team chunking heavily through the mucky gumbo. He and the buggy came to the bend at the same time: the confrontation was sudden. The buggy team spooked, surging sideways in its harness. Will-Joe quickly heeled his nervous paint to the outside of the road. The colt rolled its eyes and acted skittish, shuffling back tight against the rope.

The buggy's occupants were a hardscrabble rancher and his wife, both beefy and red-faced. The rancher swore at his skittery team and cracked his whip. They lunged into the harness and pulled on; Will-Joe held both his animals steady as the buggy swung past.

'That Injun smell,' he heard the wife mutter, 'wa'n't it, Abel?'

'Yeh.' Without turning his head, the rancher spat across his arm toward Will-Joe. 'The smell. It always sets 'em off.'

They were past him; Will-Joe heeled the paint lightly into motion again. If he hadn't forgotten long ago how to smile, he would have smiled now. Funny how he kept forgetting: that smell business was a two-way thing.

The road made a couple more ragged switchbacks through the dense timber that mantled the lower edges of the range, then Spurlock was suddenly plain through a thinning scatter of trees. A sluggish ribbon of street divided the town roughly centerwise. Stores flanked it, buildings of rough-sawed boards elbowing against old shacks of crumbling mud.

4

For at this place desert met high country; lumber and adobe mingled together as the Anglo and Mexican inhabitants did not. The best frame houses, set close together on an offside street, belonged to Anglo businessmen. The Mexes, as usual, were clustered in a haphazard Mextown south of the commercial district. The new Baptist church, painted white as its parish, was spanking-bright in the sun; its spire dominated the town. A humble 'dobe housed the Spanish mission established here nearly a hundred years before an Anglo had set foot in the country.

Will-Joe pulled up, reluctance again cold in his belly. After a moment, though, he urged the paint forward with his moccasined heels. He could skirt east of the street and its flanking block of buildings, and he did. Today he hadn't come to town on business.

The schoolhouse was set in a cottonwood park a few hundred yards south of town. Will-Joe had timed his arrival for the hour that school would let out. As he finished his circuit of the town and swung back onto the road, he passed the kids trooping down it, talking and yelling, running singly or lagging in groups. The schoolhouse, little more than a rude log shack, stood by itself in a sunny glade. Mounted on the roof was a big brass bell, a memento of steamer days on the Colorado River. The flat sunslant hit fire from its polished curve; some student had the job of keeping it rust-free, rubbed to a shine.

Will-Joe swung down at the tie rail set off in the cottonwood shade a little ways from the building, looping his reins around it. As he undid the colt's leadrope, a brown-faced boy came out on the porch, arms full of blackboard erasers. He dumped them on the steps and banged them together by pairs, chalk dust flying.

Will-Joe stood motionless, watching the boy. Seeing himself a few years ago, worshipfully lingering after class (he had bloodied another boy's nose for the privilege) to run all the after-school errands for Miss Bethany: sweeping floor, fetching firewood, cleaning blackboard erasers, doing little things that needed doing.

Miss Bethany came out on the porch as the boy was scooping up the dusted erasers.

'Thank you, Carlos. I think that will do for today. You may as well run along home ... nothing else that wants tending to.'

The boy's face tipped up; Will-Joe could picture the disappointment in it. 'Nothing, Miss Bethany?'

She smiled. 'No, Carlos. Not a blessed thing.'

Carlos went inside to replace the erasers, in a moment reappearing to cross the yard at a run. Miss Bethany walked to the edge of the porch and delicately stretched her arms. Her gaze strayed to the cottonwoods and the tie rail.

'Why—Will-Joe!' With surprise and

pleasure.

He started forward. The colt backed against the rope again. *'Ho-shuh!'* The sharp word and his tug got the animal moving. Leading him, Will-Joe crossed the scuffed dust of the yard to the porch and halted by the bottom step. He held out the rope.

'Will-Joe . . . why what is this?'

'The white colt. He is a gift. He's yours.'

'But . . . mine?' She flattened a hand against her shirt-waist below her throat. 'A gift for me? But why, Will-Joe?'

He let his hand and the rope drop to his side, looking at her. 'You don't remember?'

'No, I'm afraid . . . oh, the colt! Yes, of course I remember. But you can't mean . . .'

'I caught him. I have trained him, I have rough-broke him. Now he's yours.'

It had been a Saturday afternoon eight months ago. Miss Bethany had ridden up to his camp in the hills. He rarely had visitors, and he hadn't seen his former teacher in nearly a year. Having heard about his horse-trapping, she had come up to see for herself. Abashed and pleased by her interest, he'd taken her to one of his horse traps, a canyon with a brush wall and gate across its mouth.

Then the white colt had appeared suddenly. He had stood profiled on a ridge a few hundred yards away and his creamy coat had been burnished silver by the sun.

'Oh!' Miss Bethany had clapped her hands.

7

'What a beauty!'

'He'll be yours,' Will-Joe had promised.

She had laughed, forgetting that her solemn ex-pupil never joked.

It had meant months of patient training and waiting and watching, a half-dozen abortive tries at driving the colt into a trap. And when finally he'd succeeded, he couldn't remember a longer or tougher stint at training down the spirit of a captured mustang.

'He is yours,' Will-Joe repeated.

'Oh I couldn't . . . I couldn't, Will-Joe. He's yours, you went to all that trouble, and I really never thought—' She stopped, seeing his eyes. 'Yes. A gift. Of course.'

She took the rope from him, eyes shining. 'Oh. Oh Will-Joe, here—' She came down off the porch and took him by the shoulders and kissed his cheek and stepped back, laughing.

He stood rooted and looked at her, his insides puddling. He wondered if what he felt showed in his face, and he hoped not and also hoped it did. He veiled his eyes.

'I'm glad you like the gift.'

'He's beautiful.'

She walked slowly to the colt, who swung his head away from her strangeness, the primness of starched white waist and dark skirt and delicate scent of verbena. 'He is beautiful,' she said softly and reached, touching the colt's satiny rippling shoulder with her fingertips. She lightly moved her fingers and he didn't stir.

Beautiful. That was the horse. The word didn't do Bethany McAllister justice . . .

He had thought the very same that day three years ago when Miss Bethany and her husband, Dennis McAllister, had arrived in Spurlock. Will-Joe had come to town that day to dicker his first sale of horses. Just a few months before, he'd left his mother's people to go mustanging on his own—a wiry untried urchin determined to be beholden to no one. Weeks of backbreaking work had netted him six stringy mustangs; rough-breaking the lot, he'd had the daylights battered out of him. Today he'd brought them to town and a stock dealer, only to get what he considered badly stung on the horse-trading.

He'd been standing in the archway of the livery barn, jingling the double-eagles in his pocket and bitterly staring out through a driving rain at the white man's town, waiting for the cloudburst to stop so he could leave this hated place. A creaking prairie schooner had come sloughing down the mud-channeled street and wheeled into the livery archway. A hardscrabble outfit on its last legs: the flapping canvas was patched and grimy, the horses old and gaunted-up, their ancient harness held together by wire and rawhide.

'You. Kid. Give us a hand here.'

The man was unimpressive; Will-Joe barely heard his rough order. His eyes were all for the woman on the seat beside him. She was in her

9

early twenties, tall, almost as tall as a man, but graceful and lovely as a spring willow. Her skin was like new cream, a brushing of color in her cheeks from the coldness of rain dewing her skin. Her hair was red-gold, shading to darkness of auburn and highlighting to sudden gold even in this gloomy light.

Mustering enough aplomb to go along with the man's mistaking him for the hostler, Will-Joe had helped him unhitch and see to the team. Afterward, when the rain had slackened, he had helped carry their luggage to the hotel. McAllister had tipped him expansively. A dollar. Well above what the couple could afford, from their shabby clothes. Will-Joe had wordlessly accepted the money, then turned to leave. Miss Bethany had stopped him with a word.

'Do you live here?'

'No. In mountain.' He had moved his arm vaguely north. 'Catchem horse. Tradem here.'

'I see.'

No flicker of surprise. No remonstrations about his youth. Just a friendly and beautiful smile that said she understood. Will-Joe's heart had flip-flopped: he'd have thrown himself under wagon wheels for her.

'I will be the new teacher,' she had said. 'Would you like to come to school? I'd like to see you there.'

He'd been older than the others in Miss Bethany's first class. And the only Navajo

10

among a conglomeration of Anglo and Mexican children. For two years he had doggedly pursued his studies, eking a living meantime by such odd jobs as he could pick up.

But in all the times he had seen Miss Bethany, the picture of how she had looked that rain-swept day had stayed most vivid in his mind. Until today: her standing in the sun with her fingers brushing the white colt's shoulder, sun's goldfire in her hair, grave eyes full of pleasure.

'He's a wonderful gift. Thank you again . . . thank you so much, Will-Joe.'

'Maybe he will cost too much to keep,' Will-Joe said. 'But then you can sell him.'

'I will not! I'll never sell him. Mr Rodriguez at the stable is a friend . . . he'll put the colt up for me.'

Will-Joe had known as much. Nearly everyone in Spurlock was in Miss Bethany's debt one way or another. Beyond the meager salary they paid her for teaching their children, people owed her for scores of favors. The sick mother who needed someone to sit up with her croup-ailing child, the unlettered line rider who wanted a letter written home, the retarded child of a peon who needed special teaching: they'd all learned to know and love Bethany McAllister in a special way.

He felt the gentle probe of her glance against his face. 'How are old John Thunder and Rainbow Girl? Do you see them often?'

11

'No. Not in a long time.'

He didn't want to talk about old Adakhai whom the whites called John Thunder, or Adakhai's skinny granddaughter. Miss Bethany seemed just faintly amused, and he did not want that either.

'I'll take the colt to the stable for you. He will have to learn to eat grain and be fat.'

'He won't get fat, that I promise. I'll exercise him ... or have one of the boys do it.' She relinquished the lead-rope to him, then added, gently reproving: 'I know you've been in town twice since I visited your camp ... and you didn't come to see me.'

'I am sorry.' He hesitated. 'When I come again, we will talk.'

'Yes. A good long talk.'

She chatted awhile longer, mentioning pupils from Will-Joe's days at the school, what they were doing now. Will-Joe wasn't interested. Among his schoolmates he'd been the different one, always strange to them, shut out of their childish games. Enough to just watch Miss Bethany talk, the grave smile that reached her eyes more than her lips.

When the good-byes were said, he mounted his paint and, leading the colt, headed toward town and the stable.

A rider was coming down the road. Will-Joe had no trouble identifying the man even from a distance. Sheriff Ulring. He felt a faint chill on his spine.

Just seeing that big lean wolf of a man always had the same effect on him. *Tsi Tsosi*—Yellow Hair—was the name the Navajos had given Ulring. A fiercely warlike people till their defeat at Canyon de Chelly, the Navajos feared none of the worst elements in nature or men. Still, they feared this white man. He went out of his way to be hard on Mexicans and Indians; any who transgressed the law, any he was even suspicious of, could look for no mercy from him.

Ulring was close now, his eyes slitting coldly in the shadow of his hatbrim. They were strange eyes; their blue was ice-blue. Something stark, quick, restless prowled in them.

'Howdy, boy.'

Will-Joe nodded, a puppet-string jerk of his head, and kept his face stony as he rode past the sheriff. He felt the same as the rest did about Ulring. He was different from other men. And somehow more ominous than any force in nature.

Riding in the warm sun, Will-Joe shivered.

*   *   *

Frank Ulring rode toward the schoolhouse, his mood dense and unquiet. Behind the hard intensity of his thoughts, he wondered idly what that siwash kid had been doing at the school. What was his name?—Will-Joe something.

Cantrell, that was it, son of a squawman, so they said. Another of Bethany's proud protégés.

Ulring's broad mouth twisted faintly. She picked up all kinds, Bethany did. Going out of her way, for Christ's sake, to coddle the children of pepperguts and siwashes. Let her hear of some clan of hill trash, white, Mexican or Indian, living back in the middle of nowhere, the kids growing up half-wild and illiterate—nothing for it but Bethany must give up a holiday to ride to their place and ask, exhort, plead that they send their slew of dirty-mouthed brats to school. She'd even offer to put them up in town at her own expense. In fact she'd been trying unsuccessfully for two years to get the county fathers to build a dormitory in Spurlock for the area's underprivileged children and foot the bill for boarding and feeding them.

What a bushel of goddam nonsense.

He ought to know. He, Ulring, hadn't been born to the kind of position and respect he now claimed. And nobody, by God, had coddled him into it. He'd pulled himself up from the literal gutter by his bootstraps, and he was damned proud of it. The influential treated him as an equal, the poor but law-abiding called him Mr Ulring and talked soft to his face, the ne'er-do-wells tiptoed wide of him. The troublemakers knew him better than any—they understood the line he drew, knew

14

he drew it hard and tight and would sniff them out like a birddog if they toed across it.

Ulring kept an orderly county. Not that the law was his creed. He was the creed. The Law. Frank Ulring was The Law in Grafton County.

The lawful majority knew it too—and remembered what the region had been six short years ago, before he had come to Spurlock: a mountainous refuge for half the killers, rustlers, and robbers in the territory. Ulring had sized up the situation and seen it at once for the main chance it was. He'd been a lot of things in his thirty years: shotgun guard, bounty hunter, range war warrior, railroad detective, Army scout. Troubleshooting was his work, his life, but a man had to look to his future. With county elections coming up, Ulring had run for sheriff, told the voters in no uncertain terms exactly what he'd do and how he'd do it, and had beaten the aging, cautious incumbent in a walk. In a few months the scum had been cleaned out, dead or moved on for reasons of health. Ulring had kept it that way. The lawful majority might mutter about his methods, they might search their souls at random moments—but when ballot-marking time rolled around, they did a little thinking back and forgot their misgivings.

Ulring left his rawboned sorrel at the tie rail and crossed the yard, his spurs chinking softly, just a little awkward in the tall cowman's boots that took some of the catfooted grace from his

15

walk. Even so, he moved softly and easily for a big man. Inches over six feet, he was whittle-hipped and wedge-shouldered with long arms and large powerful hands. He had the rugged prow-nosed just-short-of-handsome features of his Norwegian ancestors; wind and sun had put a ruddy russet burn on his fair skin.

He stepped onto the porch and halted by the propped-open door, looking down past the rows of crude wooden desks to the front of the room. Bethany was sitting at her desk, head bent over some papers she was marking. A finger of sunlight from the west window made a blazing halo of her hair.

'Come in, Frank,' she said without looking up.

Ulring came down the aisle, the desks and benches like toys beside his bulk. Entering the schoolhouse always made him feel—not uncomfortable, he was superior to social unease—but bearlike and out of place. His own learning had been picked up in odd scraps at odd times. He had learned his ciphering by keeping range tallies on a saddle string; he'd gotten glimmerings of how to read by studying labels on cans at chuckwagons. Later on he had borrowed books and, by slow and painful degrees, had mastered the printed word.

Bethany laid her papers aside and smiled up at him. 'I never have to look to see you coming. The spurs—I always know. How are you, Frank?'

'Middling.'

Ulring settled one hip on the corner of her desk and glanced down at her copy of *McGuffey's Fifth Eclectic Reader*. He picked it up and let it fall open in his hands. ' "*The Mariner's Dream*," ' he read aloud.

> ' "In slumbers of midnight the sailor boy lay;
> His hammock swung loose at the sport of the wind;
> But watch-worn and weary, his cares flew away,
> And visions of happiness danced o'er his mind." '

He shut the book and laid it aside, and recited the next stanza from memory:

> ' "He dreamed of his home, of his dear native bowers,
> And pleasures that waited on life's merry morn;
> While Memory each scene gayly covered with flowers
> And restored every rose, but secreted the thorn." '

Bethany smiled. 'You can't surprise me any more, Frank. I wish you wouldn't try. You make the teacher feel inadequate.'

'Habit,' Ulring chuckled.

17

It was a bantering custom between them. Ulring enjoyed it—the same way, he supposed, that a highly athletic kid enjoyed showing off for his girl by doing handstands on a board fence. But Ulring had never learned physical prowess; he was born with it. What he enjoyed flexing for Bethany were the painfully developed muscles of his mind—but only for her.

'Met the Cantrell kid coming up the road.' He slanted his blond brows at her, mildly questioning. 'Thought he "graduated."'

'Oh—he brought me the colt. Did you see him? A gift. Will-Joe was taking him to the stable.'

Ulring smiled gravely. 'Apple for teacher, eh? Surprises me—from that kid. Surly cuss.'

'Really, Frank—you don't know him.'

'And can't say I care to.'

She picked up a pencil and frowned at it. 'Frank—' She was choosing her words. 'I'd think that you, of all people, would be sympathetic to someone like Will-Joe.'

'Look, Beth. I've nothing against the underprivileged—your word. But people like that—'

'Indians—Mexicans?'

Ulring scowled faintly, smiling too. 'You're putting words in my mouth. All right—them mostly. It's true and you know it. Education is wasted on them. Those people have no future—no sense of future time. Sure they

18

work well—when they work. And blow every cent on payday. Let some shirttail relative's third cousin throw a fiesta and you may not see 'em for a week. A white man, now. Not to puff my own crop, but I did pull myself—'

'Bootstraps. I know.' Flecks of greenfire sparked her eyes. 'But that's it, Frank. You're a white man. With all the legal and social advantages, the educational and financial opportunities that means. All right, you're a hard worker, so is Will-Joe Cantrell. He's intelligent. Quite as independent as you are. Ambitious, too. Yet he can never improve his station a whit—because he's half-Indian.'

'Maybe.' Ulring kept the disbelief in his tone mild. 'Anyway I didn't drop in to discuss the red brethren. What I wanted to ask—you think Dennis might be interested in hiring on with me?'

The abrupt question made her blink. 'Hiring on? I don't understand. Do you want him for . . .?'

She didn't finish. Didn't have to. The prime specimen she'd chosen as a husband hadn't held a steady job since the day of their arrival in Spurlock. Dennis McAllister's days were spent hanging around the saloons and cajoling an occasional stranger into a card game. He picked up occasional work at swamping stables, sweeping up in stores, running flunky's errands. And spent the rest of his time talking about 'getting something better.'

19

'I want him for a regular job.' Ulring shifted his hip on the desk and crossed his hands on his knees. 'Steady hours, fairly good pay ... it'll keep him jumping.'

'Oh, I see.' She gave a wry, deprecating smile. 'Claude is quitting you.'

She meant Claude Warhoon, the shiftless, grinning fumbler who served as Ulring's jailer, kept his office tidy, fetched his coffee and otherwise attended to the details that Ulring couldn't be bothered with.

'Not Claude. He knows a good thing when he has it.' Ulring smiled patiently. 'What I'm offering Dennis is a *job*—as my deputy.'

Her eyes were incredulous. 'Frank, you're not serious.'

'Dead serious. Job's gotten too big for me to handle. I need a man.'

'But Dennis ...! Frank, he's not a gunman—not a fighter. He's in no way cut out for that sort of work. You know he isn't!'

'Look.' Ulring bent a little, thumping a finger on the desk. 'Grafton County's growing up fast, Beth. The outlaws and floaters, all that scum, have been cleaned out—'

'Thanks to you.'

'Don't interrupt, teacher. People are flocking in by droves every year. They see this as a good place to settle, to farm and ranch, to raise families. And it's only begun. The country will grow, we'll all grow with it. Even my job is getting civilized—too tame already for my

20

taste. There's all the paperwork piling up. Claude can't handle it and I hate to. Dennis can be a big help there. Dozens of other duties falling to my lot that he could take care of and never touch trouble ... like riding miles to serve papers on some harmless squatter.'

'It wouldn't be fair.' Bethany bit her lip and lowered her eyes. 'Not fair to you. He's never held any job for more than a week or so. He'll disappoint you, Frank—and me again. It's happened too often.'

'I'll take the chance,' Ulring said. 'Will you?'

'Yes. You knew I would, didn't you? Thank you.' Her eyes came up. 'It seems I'm everlastingly thanking you—for one favor or another. How many times in the past three years have you helped us out, Frank?'

'I never keep count,' Ulring said idly. 'Don't you.'

Her hand was at the bosom of her waist fingering the gold watch-pin there—a relic of gentility—and his glance touched the gentle curve of breast beneath it. She wasn't a small woman, she was more robust than ethereal, yet dainty was the word for her. She had an inbred delicacy that poverty couldn't erase, a fine-trained strength of bloodline blended with a spring-blossom fragility; it made a fever in him that ranged far beyond any raw sensuality.

Fever. Was that the word? Lust, in any case, was too harsh a term. He had known lust too often to be mistaken about the difference.

21

What he felt for this woman stood alone in all Frank Ulring's experience.

It had been that way from the day the McAllisters had arrived in Spurlock. That evening Ulring had entered the hotel dining room at the usual supper hour, and the two of them were at a table. Bethany's beauty had been a flame against the drab room and the day's gray-rain gloom. Ulring had gone promptly over to introduce himself and offer his services. A few minutes of conversation had made the picture clear: the loyal wife and the weakling husband. A beautiful hopeful woman wedded to a permanent failure.

In almost the same minute he'd known something else. Bethany McAllister was going to be his.

He'd made the decision just that suddenly, not feeling a jot of surprise about it, just a certainty as quietly absolute as the massive roof beam of a barn being settled into place.

Once he'd decided his course, though, Ulring had felt his way into the situation with infinite care. He'd cultivated Dennis as much as he had Bethany; he'd found them a house to live in, established their credit with local merchants, smoothed their way into the community. While piece by piece he was putting together the history of their crumbling relation. It seemed promising. McAllister's vapid ways were steadily running whatever his wife might still feel for him into the ground.

22

Meantime he, Ulring, always managed to be on hand at the times when Bethany needed a friend most—just a good friend to talk with.

The possibility of failure hadn't occurred to him. Why should it? He'd enjoyed plenty of casual success with women: it might take time, but in the end Bethany would turn naturally to him.

Nearly three years. And it hadn't worked out that way.

He hadn't reckoned with the stubborn depth of her loyalty. There couldn't be much, if anything, left of her feeling for McAllister; still Ulring had come to realize that Bethany would cling to her marriage vows till all hell froze over. He knew it without her ever quite saying so. She'd never complained of her lot nor (till he'd mentioned the deputy's job just now) said a word that might be construed as critical of her husband. Instinct had warned Ulring not to press the issue.

Once realization had come, he hadn't hesitated an instant in considering his next step. It had come to him as easily and surely as his decision to take another man's wife.

But he had to go even more carefully. He needed a plan. Foolproof. And he had one.

'Well, I'll be moseying, Beth.' He rose, the skirt of his fringed buckskin coat peeling away from the desktop. 'You tell Dennis; let him sleep on it. I'll drop by in the morning.'

'Thank you again, Frank—for everything.'

She stood up, giving him her hand. Ulring took it, bowed slightly, gravely, and then tramped out. He walked to the tie rail, mounted, and rode back toward town.

Jogging down the dappled dust of the road, he grinned. A mere shaping of his broad lips: the effect was as cold as his eyes.

Till death us do part.

Sure as hell, he thought. And let the grin widen till his big teeth showed.

CHAPTER TWO

Even at midsummer, the chill of high country dawn reached Bethany bone-deep as she padded in slippered feet to the kitchen and lighted the heap of kindling shavings she had laid in the big range the night before. She folded her arms across the front of her gray wrapper and shivered, pacing the floor while she waited for the blaze to take. She could hear Dennis beginning to stir in their room off the tiny *sala*; he had come in last night with a load that would stagger a moose and she'd had the devil's time rousing him to half-wakefulness this morning.

The room wasn't much: Frank Ulring had gotten it at a bargain from the son of an ancient saddlemaker, the old man having died a month before the McAllisters arrived in Spurlock. It had been a combination home and shop; a smell of cured leather still clung faintly to the old rooms. The 'dobe walls were two feet thick with a heavy earthen roof. The pieces of hand-carved furniture were smoky-dark with age; Navajo blankets made passable rugs on the cold pack-clay floors.

The fire was building nicely; she stoked it with cedar lengths from the woodbox. Dennis came in; he hadn't troubled to shave, and the pepper-salt stubble on his jaws darkened the cheek hollows she'd once thought ascetic. He was slender, of average height, but looked oddly smaller in rough wool pants and shirt, cheap durable clothing he was forced to wear in lieu of the expensive broadcloth suits he'd once favored.

'Christ, what time is it?' He sat down at the table, groaned, and ran his hands backward through his hair. 'I didn't get four hours' sleep, for God's sake.'

'Whose fault is that?' Bethany stood sideways to him, not glancing at him as she ladled Triple X into a pot of water.

'Look, I pick up a few dollars hanging late at the tables, it all helps. Not as though you earn it all.'

Bethany didn't think it worth commenting that he lost more than he won or that the 'few dollars' he added to the household funds were withdrawn twice over by the end of each month to pay for his losings and his liquor.

She merely said: 'How much did you win last night?'

No answer.

She looked at him. His head was down, elbows on the table and steepled thumbs grooving his lower lip. How handsome he had seemed when she was a seventeen-year-old Boston Belle!

A gentleman born, too: well-dressed, fine-spoken, beautifully mannered. Neither she nor her parents had guessed—nor bothered to check, worse luck—on what was common knowledge among Tidewater Virginia gentry: that the McAllisters' aristocratic blood had run thin a generation back. Dennis's father's lack of financial acumen had dissolved most of the McAllister fortune; Dennis and his wastrel brothers had finished the job. To Bethany's parents, the thirty-year-old Southerner had seemed a prime catch for a marriageable daughter; her bluestocking soul had shivered deliciously to his soft southern voice and flamboyant elegance. All parties willing, the wedding had been quickly arranged and swiftly consummated. It would take only a painful week or so for Bethany to learn that Dennis McAllister was only a pale copy of what he'd seemed: a man who caricatured genuine qualities with perfect aplomb because they did not come naturally to him.

Well, she told herself with dreary self-mockery, you were just young, my dear.

The years since had been one pattern of one cloth. Indifference, incompetence, his temper that flared and died, would cause Dennis to leave whatever halfway decent jobs he could obtain. There was always a new will-o'-the wisp for him to chase: one time it might be a mine in Colorado; another time, cotton lands in the Mississippi basin. Whatever his current enthusiasm, he would always rub her nerve with his sulky petulance till she'd give up and accede to his wishes. Then they'd move on again, each time a little poorer in goods and pride.

Finally, though, it had been Bethany who, after hearing of Spurlock's need for a teacher, had insisted on coming here. And in the small log school here she'd found her anchor and her cause: something she could believe in, cherish, fight for. When Dennis, restless once more, had found her immovable against all his sulkings and blusterings, he'd surlily resigned himself to living in her shadow. And subjecting her to an occasional spate of malice.

He said suddenly, irritably: 'When did Ulring say he'd come by?'

'He didn't. But it'll be early, knowing Frank.'

'And you do know him, don't you, my dear?'

Oh God, she thought wearily. She finished breaking an egg into the spitting bacon grease, then turned to face him. 'I won't ask you what that's supposed to mean. I know. And you know exactly how false it is.'

27

His eyes fell. 'Sure,' he muttered. 'Does he?'

'That's too deep for me, I'm afraid.'

'I doubt it. I doubt it would be even for a stupid woman. And you're far from stupid, Beth.'

'Sometimes I've wondered.'

He laughed. 'You know as well as I why Ulring's done all he has . . . this house, all the favors. Hell, the whole town knows. And now a tailor-made job for old Dennis. Well, well.'

It took an effort to keep her voice steady. 'Perhaps you'd tell me what all you people know—if anything.'

'Why, there's always talk, my dear. You know that. Oh, everyone's sure you're a tower of rectitude, no less. But the sheriff, now. Folks aren't the least shy about speculating as to why Ulring's favored the McAllisters so much. It's all on your account, of course.'

'That's rubbish.'

Dennis gave a sober nod, somehow managing, without twitching a muscle of his face, to convey the effect of a dirty-mouthed leer. She set his food before him, clattering the dishes down in her anger. She was used to this sort of thing from him, but usually it came as a veiled form of innuendo. And he hadn't made a reference this direct to Ulring before.

Maybe he hadn't cared before. Now he'd be working under Ulring—in a job that Ulring had offered through Bethany, not to him directly. Though Dennis couldn't afford to turn down

28

the offer, it must rankle him deeply. For he still had pride of a sort. God knew why, but he did.

Bethany felt rankled herself, quite upset in fact, and she knew why. There was a good deal more than simple pique behind Dennis's words. Of course there was. Other people than Ulring had given Dennis work merely to oblige her. But she'd be a fool to suppose for a moment that it was the same as with Frank Ulring, who never did favors out of compassion or even obligation. His reason, apparently, was so transparent that—if you could believe Dennis—people were talking.

Not that Ulring had ever taken any kind of liberty with her in either his speech or his manner. In the many times they had visited, he had kept his words and glances strictly and pleasantly impersonal, never a trace of boldness. And still his force and his boldness were just under the surface, a raw flame. When he looked at her, it was as a man looked at a woman. A more-than-attractive woman, a special woman. And that was how she always felt under even his casual glance: womanly.

The feeling had made her increasingly uneasy. It got to her more than she liked to admit. It was no way for a married woman, a respectable schoolteacher, to think or feel . . .

Someone tapped at the kitchen door; she opened it.

Ulring stood on the porch, hat in hand. His white-blond mane of hair and thick spike of

29

beard gave him the look of a Viking corsair; his teeth were big and white when he smiled.

'Morning, Beth. May I come in?'

'Good morning, Frank. Of course ... do have some coffee.'

She went to the stove to pour it, glad she could put her back to the room a moment. Her face felt slightly flushed, as if she'd been caught with her thoughts showing. Ulring settled his bulk in a creaking chair, smiled his thanks as she set the cup before him, and glanced at Dennis.

'How's the job sound?'

'What's the difference?' Dennis stirred his shoulders vaguely. 'I need it.'

'You don't sound so sure.'

'I'm sure. I guess you were sure too.'

Ulring nodded impersonally. He raised his cup of scalding-hot coffee, drank it off and set the cup down. 'If you're ready, let's hustle.'

Bethany said: 'Frank, surely you've time for some breakfast.'

'Thanks, I've eaten. I want to show Dennis what his duties are, get him broken into the paperwork, and I've other things to handle. Be a busy day.'

Dennis gulped his food, pulled on his coat and he and Ulring went out. Bethany watched them from the window, the two men side by side as they headed down the street. And watching, felt her mind draw unwilling comparisons.

30

Why not? Was it wrong to feel gratified—and yes, womanly and wanted—because a handsome man had found her pleasing? Did a mere feeling or two make her an adulteress? Her puritan ancestors would have said so: her conscience couldn't help groping for vindication. Memory ran a bitter eye back over the years with Dennis McAllister: his weaknesses, his little abuses, his petty jealousies. What was there left?

Nothing. Dennis had killed it off himself. By his own efforts—or lack of effort. It had been a long time since she'd felt anything for him but pity. She bowed her head and closed her eyes, clenching her hands on the window-sill. Even pity, she was finding, had its limits . . .

*   *   *

Claude Warhoon emerged from the cell block behind the sheriff's office, taking a few more idle swipes at the floor with his broom. Claude was a towering young man with a long, amiable, lantern-jawed face and hair so pale as to be nearly white. He halted in the center of the office, leaned on the broom, thumb-snapped one of his galluses, and looked at Ulring.

'She's all swept out, Frank. Anything else this morning?'

Ulring was seated at his desk, reading. He glanced up. 'I reckon not. You holding down another job?'

31

'Well, Rodriguez over at the stable asked if I could swamp out his place.' Claude snickered. 'Seeing Dennis ain't got that job no more.'

Dennis, sitting at a scarred table and bent grimly over some papers spread on its top, didn't even look up.

'All right with me,' Ulring said. 'Nothing else wants doing here. Just see you get back by noon to feed the prisoners.'

'Yes, sir.'

Claude put away his broom, clamped on his hat and went out. The office was silent except for the quick scratching of Dennis's pen. Ulring idly pulled out his watch and noted the time—less than two hours to twelve—and thought: old Anse ought to be barging in here directly.

A faint impatience rose like vapor in his belly. Not the impatience of second-thought panic or even of irritation at the delay—just the cool hackle-bristling excitement he'd always felt at any job in prospect, an eagerness to get on with it.

He dropped his gaze to the open book before him: the *Institutes* of Gaius. The classic handbook of Roman law was typical of the curious byways into which Ulring's questing mind led him. Difficult reading was a good thing before a job; it braced and sharpened his wits, and ordinary qualms of anticipation never distracted him because he'd never known them.

He lost himself once more in the old Roman scholar's fine-spun syllogisms. It may have

32

been five minutes or fifteen minutes later that boots scraped on the walk outside and the office door was pushed open. Anse Burris, who owned a one-loop outfit upvalley a ways, came in like a raw wind. His face was set against the pain that ravaged his wizened body as he tramped over to Ulring's desk and halted truculently.

'I got some cattle missing, Frank.' One of the few not impressed by Ulring's authority or his reputation, he stared the lawman straight in the eye. 'You want to get off your big shiny badge and come look?'

Ulring closed his book and leaned back in his chair. 'Maybe you better give me the story.'

Burris eased his tortured body some by leaning both fists on the desk. His skin was the polished brown of old oak leaves; his hair and whiskers were frosted by the years and hard living. 'There's a meadow on the edge of my top range, Seldon's Park they call it, you know the place.'

'I know it.'

'Yestiday I had a jag of cattle up there. This morning they're gone.'

Ulring moved his shoulders. 'Cal Bender's place is just east of yours. Were the brands haired over? Cal might have pushed 'em down with his stuff by mistake.'

'Them brands was clipped smooth as a baby's ass. Sure they was pushed, but not down by Cal's. They was drove north toward Lacy.'

'You trail 'em?'

'Hell, I ain't followed no rough trail since I taken a fall off that spooky roan last summer. I wouldn't make it acrost the first ridge.'

Ulring steepled his fingers, nodding slowly. 'Lacy, hunh? That's a hardcase mining town, over the county line too. By now those cows could be butchered, the hides buried and the quarters hung up in a mineshaft somewhere.'

'Horseshit, man! I know that. Nothing to keep you from trailing 'em far as the line ... could be they never got drove across.'

'Reckon I figured that for myself, Anse.' Ulring rose, walked to the hatrack and took down his pearl-gray Stetson. He looked at Dennis who'd left off writing to take in the conversation. 'Want to come?'

Surprise washed over Dennis's face. 'Me? Sure ... but all this paperwork—'

'Leave it today, no rush. There's more than one side to law work ... you won't see much of this side, but you ought to get some idea of it.'

'Do I take along a gun?'

Dennis couldn't keep the eager note from his voice, and Ulring almost smiled: like any bored and jaded man, McAllister was on edge for some sort of excitement, any sort. He'd expected as much—but if his new deputy had expressed disinterest, he'd have made the suggestion an order.

'Sure,' Ulring said carelessly. He took a Winchester from the gunrack and tossed it to

34

Dennis. 'Shells in my desk, top drawer. Fetch a box for me too.'

Smiling a little, he chose his own favorite rifle from the rack and rubbed his palm along its scarred stock . . .

At the livery Ulring claimed his own mount and ordered a horse saddled for Dennis. They joined old Burris, waiting in his buckboard at the tie rail, and the three rode out on the north road. The spring day was warm and full of the strong resinous smell of sun-touched pines. Anse guided the buckboard carefully over the stiff mud ruts, still only half-thawed from last night's plunging cold. Dennis rode up beside the wagon; Ulring jogged about twenty feet behind, slouched easily into his horse's gait. His eyes were half-lidded, slanting against Dennis's back: the faint smile came back to his lips.

It would work. No reason it shouldn't. It would be easy.

In an hour they achieved the headquarters of Burris's Cross T outfit. It was a modest house with a few outbuildings set between some shouldering hills. Burris's wife invited them in for coffee, but old Anse said: 'Save it till they're back, 'Manda. I want 'em to hustle on that trail.'

He got a horse from his corral, painfully mounted and led the way past the sheds and corral going up a gradual slope into deep timber. Hitting the roiling cut of Jewel Creek on its journey out of the peaks, they followed it upstream awhile. When its flow bent sharply toward higher country, they left it and followed a game trail that curved down out of the shadowed timber. They came out above Seldon's Park. Off to their left, at the head of the meadow, rose a hill of crumbling granite.

Burris pulled up his horse and pointed.

'You see that hill. First thing I do each morning is tramp up here way we come and get up on that hill. Can see clear to two sides of my propity line from here. That's wherefrom I spotted them cows was missing.'

Ulring nodded. He knew of Anse's habit of rising with first light and making a slow circle of his place, finally coming up on this promontory. Half the county knew of it. After his crippling fall last year, for all the pain it cost him, Anse had continued this custom; nearly everyone knew that too. Anse had been bound to spot the missing cattle this morning . . .

They put their horses across the meadow, Anse leading the way. New grass was poking up through last year's dead gray-buff cover. A pair of mountain jays skimmed low ahead of the riders, blue long-tailed flashes in the sun before they dipped up and away. Anse halted at the meadow's north edge where tall spruce had provided a windbreak that had caused the snow to pile in deep ridges. Here the meadow tilted, causing the melting snow to carve a gully in the soil. Where the end of the gully funneled out into the grass, a broad delta had formed.

The damp clay was trampled full of cattle prints, and among them Anse pointed out the clear tracks of a single horse.

'There was a dozen cows here. You can see for yourself they was drove off. Just to make sure, I rode over to Bender's after I left here. Cal pushed all his stuff down on the new grass two days ago, he says. He ain't got a beef on his place that come inside seventy pounds of these three-year-olds of mine. Them was my cows was taken.'

'All right,' Ulring said. 'You showed us. Go on home.'

'There's plenty trails he could of taken besides the one to Lacy,' Burris pointed out. 'Don't kite off the wrong way on a guess. See you cut their sign right.'

'Go on home, Anse. We'll cut it.'

Burris mounted again and rode back the way they'd come. Ulring walked slowly back and forth beside the wide fan of mud, pretending to scrutinize it. When he looked up again, Burris had diminished to a dot at the meadow's south edge, just disappearing in the timber. Ulring glanced at Dennis, who was sitting his horse impatiently.

'I've got all the sign pegged in my head now. I'll know it anywhere. Let's follow it.'

'You think there'll be trouble?'

Ulring shrugged. 'Always a chance. The sign says one man, but he might have friends where he's headed for. You got second thoughts?'

37

Dennis flushed. 'Hell, I'm not afraid.'

'That's fine.' Ulring showed his big teeth, grinning. 'There'll be just you and me, fella. Just you and me . . .'

CHAPTER THREE

On foot, Will-Joe was trailing a deer. He had come on its sign minutes ago and had tracked it to the bare crown of a hill. Keeping his eyes forward more than on the ground, he spotted the buck at once as he topped the hill. The animal was standing at the fringe of a pine belt that began halfway down the slope. He was frozen in place, head alert; he was gray-brown against the somber green and a web of morning sun sheened his antlers.

The buck had already got his scent, Will-Joe knew, and the animal's next, almost instantaneous move was expected: he wheeled and vanished into the wall of pines.

Moccasined and noiseless, Will-Joe went down the hillside at a sharp quick diagonal, the rifle swinging in his fist. With the wind at his back, he didn't plunge directly on the buck's trail. He hit the first pines a good hundred yards to the right of that point, then proceeded downward on a rough-guessed parallel to the deer's line of flight. He knew that the buck would watch his backtrail, probably zigzag a bit, maybe circle back into the wind before considering himself out of danger.

It was cool in the deep shade under the tall trees; molten puddles of sunlight showered the needle floor. Will-Joe was a shadow going through the shadows; he kept on the move but always checked back to see that his direction was right. His eyes were quick for any break in the trees that might show his quarry.

The pine belt thinned away and came to an end. The buck emerged from the trees at about the moment that Will-Joe did, both of them stepping into a wide-open alley between the pines and the scraggly overgrowth of piñon and cedar that covered the lower slope. Will-Joe's rifle was swinging up even as the deer moved into sight.

It was a very close shot, a quick easy shot. A neck shot that neatly broke the spinal column.

When the cloud of white powdersmoke had frayed away, the buck was down, dropped in his tracks. Mild tucks of satisfaction touched the corners of Will-Joe's mouth. He liked a clean shot, a clean kill. Usually he hunted only for the pot: rabbits and squirrels. He'd go after large game maybe twice a year, and then he scrupulously used all of the carcass—well, most of it—for one purpose or another.

He walked down to the deer and turned it belly up, anchoring it that way with a couple of good-sized rocks. Pulling his knife, he made a three-inch cut below the short ribs, slicing through skin, fat and flesh, thrusting his fingers in to hold the intestines away from the blade. He cut down to each side of the testicles and around the rectum, then tied off the ducts leading to each with rawhide strings to keep anything from leaking out. Reaching high into the abdominal cavity, he cut the diaphragm loose all around, afterward cutting out the windpipe, gullet and large arteries. A few quick slashes along the backbone and the viscera was free; he turned the carcass on its side, spilled everything out in a lake of blood, and then, with handfuls of dry grass, wiped the inside completely dry.

For Will-Joe, it had been a few minutes' casual work. He corner-tucked his lips, thinking of the white people he'd heard gripe about the strong gamy flavor of venison. Keeping your meat clean and avoiding spoilage was just a matter of dropping your kill first shot, then butchering promptly and properly. After he'd picked out the heart, liver and kidneys, Will-Joe slit the underside of the deer's jaw, pulled the tongue down through the opening and severed it near the base. All delicacies, they'd be quickly eaten: he tucked them away in a parfleche brought for the purpose. The gutted carcass, which didn't dress out over a hundred pounds, he slung across his shoulders and, grasping the legs, tramped back toward where he'd left his horse.

The meat, cut into strips and jerked, would

last him a long while; the hide and bones would come in handy, the abdominal fat would render good lard, even the hoofs would boil down to a very palatable grease. Of course old Adakhai would have verbally blistered him for abandoning intestines, blood, bladder, and excrement, each of which had its uses. But as he could cheaply buy in Spurlock all the accessory needs these would have filled, Will-Joe thought that observing the fine points of butchery was pretty pointless. ('There the white-eyes in you speaks,' Adakhai would say scornfully.) Maybe, when the meat had cooled—hanging from a tree through a chill mountain night should do it—he might pack one of the quarters down to Miss Bethany's. Another gift—and a welcome one, he guessed, at the McAllister table.

Just thinking of *her* made his young face soften a little. *Miss Bethany*. The name turned gently on his mind's tongue, gentle as spring rain.

He'd never thought of her any way but respectfully. In Will-Joe's scheme of things, she was so far above him it would be worse than disrespectful to think of her in any more personal way. It would be sacrilege. He'd read about knights of old and how they gave fealty to a lady. That was how he'd felt from the first about Miss Bethany. Seeing her again yesterday after many months had brought the old feeling back as strongly as ever.

41

Remembering her pleasure at the colt gave him pleasure all over again. Maybe gifting her with a quarter of venison so soon after was too much. People might talk. But then—white or Indian—they did anyway.

By the time he'd tramped up the hill and halfway down its other side, a twisting ache had grabbed Will-Joe's shoulders; he was starting to sweat. He shifted his burden a little and tramped doggedly on. He had left his horse back of a ridge a quarter mile on, and he could carry the carcass that far.

He reached the bottom of the hill, and, instead of going straight up over the next hill the way he'd come while tracking the deer, swung toward an east-west wash that cut through the ridges. This route would save him a little time and he needn't carry his kill up or down any more rocky slopes.

He came to the wash, climbed down its steep cutbank and began tramping east along its sandy bottom. Almost at once, though, he slowed. Then came to a stop.

The sign on the bed of the wash was plain. Maybe a dozen cows had been pushed along the shallow gully by a single rider. Will-Joe eased the deer carcass to the ground, then knelt and touched the recent tracks. They weren't more than ten hours old. The print of the horse's right front shoe, he noticed, was quite distinctive: the shoe had been built up with two caulks on the inside.

In themselves, the tracks wouldn't have excited his curiosity too much. Anyone could buy a jag of cows somewhere and haze them home. What was bothersome, these particular tracks had been made last night. Around midnight or pretty close to it. And what honest cowman trailed his beeves home at night, even by a full moon?

Will-Joe settled back on his haunches, scowling at the tracks. None of his business, was it? A half-breed learned the bitter wisdom of staying out of all white-man business, whether it was above board or underhanded.

Just suppose, though ... suppose the business happened to involve Indians? More specifically, his own people, the Navajos?

It could be, he thought worriedly.

This whole range of ridges made a firm division between the foothills and the mountainous back-country. A few years ago, Will-Joe remembered, some young Navajos with too much *toghlepai* in their bellies had run off some cows from the valley ranches and butchered them in the foothills, then packed the beef up by secret trails to the mountain plateau where Adakhai's band lived. But *Tsi Tsosi*—Sheriff Ulring—had managed to track the thieves to Adakhai's village where he'd uncovered the carelessly concealed hide of a freshly butchered steer.

Ulring had minced no words. He'd told Adakhai that he had until nightfall to deliver the guilty parties to his office at Spurlock. The warning was ignored. Next day Ulring had returned with a posse of twenty or so white men. They'd shot up the village, burned a score of hogans, collected the possessions of a dozen families in a pile and set fire to it.

This was merely to serve notice, the sheriff had told Adakhai, and the old chief had taken the hint. After that, whenever any of his young men transgressed white-man law, Adakhai had cooperated with Ulring to see that justice was meted out. And Ulring's brand of justice had quickly persuaded all renegades and would-be renegades to toe a straight and narrow line; Navajo thievery and moonshining had almost ceased to be.

Had it started up again?

Tracks of stolen cows leading back toward the mountains pointed to that uneasy possibility. The single rider's horse had been shod white-man style, but any smart Indian cow thief might ride a shod horse. Of course there was plenty of white riffraff living back in those same peaks, but Ulring's first suspicions— knowing him—would fall on the Navajos, guilty or not.

That, Will-Joe decided, made the business of a few stolen cows his business.

Slinging the deer across his shoulders again, he followed the cattle trail to the end of the wash, then left it and climbed up the right-hand slope till he came to a patch of scrub oak. His paint horse was tethered there. Will-Joe laid the carcass in a stony hollow, then used sticks to prop open the body cavity so the meat would cool faster. He trimmed some leafy branches from the scrub oak and laid them over the carcass to keep off the shifting sun and any fat-hunting jays.

With his meat safely cached, he mounted his paint and rode down to the trail. Picking up the cattle sign again, he began to follow it, riding slowly and bending sideways from his saddle.

Hopefully he'd find where the stolen cows had been taken . . . and who had taken them. Afterward he could lead the sheriff straight to the place. Then, if the thief were white or Mexican, the Navajos wouldn't suffer the blame. Should the thief prove to be Navajo, it would be a good thing that another Navajo, Will-Joe, had not only discovered and reported it, but had also led the law to the criminal . . .

*   *   *

They were crossing a shale-capped ridge when Dennis's horse slipped. Ulring had already picked his way safely across the stretch of slick and broken rock, and Dennis was following on the downslope. Abruptly his mount's hoofs skidded; the animal floundered in a stiff-legged slide for two yards before he got his foot again. A small avalanche of shale chunks and chips cascaded downward, setting up a clatter among

45

the rocks.

Ulring had pulled up below, waiting. Dennis swore, fighting his horse on a clumsy rein, finally kneeing him up beside the sheriff's.

'Make lots of noise,' Ulring said. 'If the party we're tracking is just ahead, it ought to be dandy for alerting him.'

Dennis was flushed and furious. 'It could have happened to anyone!'

'Sure. It did to you.'

They had been on the rustler trail an hour and more, and Dennis's early enthusiasm had evaporated. He was out of condition and no horseman anyway. He was nervous about what might be ahead; you could tell by his eye movements and the way he was sweating. Both men had removed their coats against the day's rising heat, but it wasn't warm enough to justify a heavy sweat.

'The hell with you!' Dennis said hotly. 'You think I don't know why you gave me this job?'

Easy on him, Ulring warned himself. You don't want him quitting cold and turning back, not after you got him this far. He made his tone reasonable: 'Ease down there, fella.'

'It's my wife, isn't it? That's your reason, isn't it, Ulring?'

Keep on talking, boy, Ulring thought. Keep talking while you still can. 'You're imagining things,' he said mildly. And chopped off the discussion by wheeling his horse and putting him away down the ridge.

Once off the shale, the trail of the stolen cattle picked up again, as Ulring had known it would. Occasionally, for Dennis's benefit, he pretended to scan the ground. Actually—since he knew where the tracks would lead and the exact route they'd follow—he paid them almost no attention.

The trail clung to the ridge shoulder for a ways, then dropped at a gentle angle into a timbered valley. It followed game trails across several more ridges, then dropped at a gradual pitch into the upper basin of the Winnetka River. A small ranch sprawled across the slope just below them, its log house and weathered outbuildings darkly squalid against the new pale green of spring grass. Heavy timber almost enclosed the place, rambling in wooded fingers to the base of the slope, then ending on the edge of a wet meadow where the river waters had backed up beyond a fringe of alders and willows. Grazing cattle dotted the meadow.

'That's Sid Leggett's place,' Ulring said almost idly. 'Well, no surprise.'

'Who's Leggett?'

'He's trash. A bummer and a swillhead. Now a cow thief.'

Ulring reached down for the rifle under his knee and snaked it from the scabbard. Dennis said in a startled voice: 'Don't you have to turn up the cows before you arrest him?'

'They're here, don't worry. Sid's going to show us where.'

Ulring kneed his horse forward and down the slope.

They rode into the yard, which was littered with rusting tin cans and empty bottles. Leggett came out on the sagging porch, a wiry feist of a man who looked as if he hadn't washed or shaved in weeks. He was shirtless, his filth-stiff trousers gallused over his dirty underwear. He carried a Winchester rifle, and it was already half-raised and loosely trained on them.

'You want something?'

'About a dozen cows,' Ulring said.

He pulled up his horse and held his rifle balanced across his pommel, making no effort to lift it. He sat his saddle in an easy half-slouch, watching Leggett with a pleasant smile. Ulring knew the man for a loner, surly and un-approachable. He had no wife nor any family except maybe for relatives back in the Tennessee hills of his birth. Nobody, Ulring thought with satisfaction, would mourn him; none would miss him.

'What in hell you talking about?' Leggett said.

'A dozen cows,' Ulring repeated. 'Their trail leads here, Sid, straight into your place. There's no other this side of the river.'

'What cows?' Leggett's face squinted into leathery lines. 'Whose?'

'Anse Burris's cows. They were drove off last night. We followed the track here.'

'Maybe you did,' Leggett said softly, 'but

48

don't you say I took 'em, mister.'

'If you didn't, you might have an idea who did.'

'Nobody took anyone's cows!' Leggett's eyes showed a jagged fray of temper. 'You see any cows around here but mine, you point 'em out. Otherwise you can drag ass off my place and that goddam quick!'

Ulring raised a hand. 'Sid, simmer down now. Nobody's accusing you. All I'm saying, the trail leads here. Those cows were trailed by one rider. Maybe it was some hard case from over Lacy way that took 'em. Maybe it was one of old John Thunder's Navajos. Whoever it was, he drove the stuff onto your range. Maybe he drove 'em clear on across it. We don't know yet.'

'Then you got your gall busting in here like God A'mighty and rough-talking a man.'

Ulring smiled. 'Well now, Sid. Could be we owe you an apology. If you didn't take those cows, you won't object to us having a look at the ones grazing yonder.'

Leggett let his rifle tip slowly downward, his eyes stony. 'There's no Cross T stuff in with mine.'

'If that's so, you'll want to cooperate. We'll look those cows over. If there's no Cross T brands mixed in and we're witnesses to the fact, nobody can accuse you, can they?'

Leggett let the gun barrel settle till it was pointed groundward. He gave a grudging nod.

'I guess—'

That was as far as he got. Ulring had only waited for him to drop his aim. Now Ulring lifted his rifle off his pommel, levering it in the same motion. When the barrel stopped moving an instant later, it was centered on Leggett's chest.

Ulring fired.

Leggett's light body was slammed back against the door-frame. He hung there for a moment and then dropped on his face across the porch, his head and one arm hanging off the edge.

Ulring turned his head. Dennis was to one side of him and a little behind him. His face was white and shocked. His starkly staring eyes moved to Ulring.

'Why did you do that?'

'You won't have to worry about it,' Ulring said.

He shifted the rifle to his left hand and picked up his reins with his right. He lightly, almost casually neck-reined his animal, quartering him around till he was full face to Dennis. He brought his right hand back to the lever of his rifle as he raised it, and then Dennis understood. His eyes silvered with terror and he began to wheel . . .

The rifle crashed. Dennis spun sideways out of his saddle and hit the ground like a bundle of rags. He rolled over once and onto his face and was still: the empty force of momentum, for he

50

was already dead.

Ulring curbed his fiddlefooting horse. He was smiling as he let his rifle ease back to the pommel. Then—somewhere in the tail of his eye, far to the upper right of his vision, he felt as much as saw a flick of color or movement.

He swung his head quickly to the side and upward, his glance running up the slope above the house and buildings.

His smile froze. His brain blanked. The woods ended a few hundred feet above the ranchyard. And sitting his horse on the open slope just below the trees—watching him, watching everything—was that breed kid. Will-Joe Cantrell.

CHAPTER FOUR

Will-Joe had followed the trail as it climbed steadily through the ridges. He wasn't surprised when it dropped off toward the Winnetka basin and Leggett's ranch. He considered Leggett white-man trash on the bottom rung; the rancher had once shot at him just for crossing a corner of his land. Emerging on the ridge flank above the place, Will-Joe stayed close to the trees as he halted to study the layout below. He'd never seen Leggett's place from the rear before, nor had he ever been this close to it.

A hog wallow of a place, it fitted its owner. But that was the least of Will-Joe's concerns. He restlessly scanned the timber, the meadow flats along the river, and the ranch headquarters again. The trail he'd been following pointed downridge and he guessed it didn't go much farther. Probably those stolen cows were down on the meadow yonder. But would Leggett be that stupid?

He gently gigged his paint into motion, moving down the ridgeslant toward the headquarters. Then the cattle sign twisted sideways almost abruptly and headed into the deeper timber. He followed it for a couple hundred yards to an opening in the trees. A dozen cows were grazing on the sparse grass between the mossy windfalls that littered the floor of this narrow glade. Will-Joe swung in close to one; before it shied away, he saw the clean-clipped brand: Cross T, Anse Burris's outfit.

A clumsy piece of thievery on Leggett's part, driving the stolen Cross T stuff to a hiding place in the timber this close to his headquarters. To Will-Joe, the trail in here seemed clear as glass. Maybe it wouldn't be, though, to a white tracker; a white man, even Sheriff Ulring, would be likely to miss more than he saw.

Will-Joe had no affection for Anse Burris, whom he knew for a crusty Indian-hater. It was almost with reluctance that he turned his paint and swung him back down the trail. The sheriff should be notified right away: with the rightful thief, Leggett, pinpointed for sure, there'd be no possibility of blame touching any Navajo.

Something, he wasn't sure what, made Will-Joe pull to a halt. He listened. Nothing but a squirrel's friskings in the limbs above broke the dappled quiet. Then he caught a distinct muffled beat of horses' hoofs on the cushiony needle turf. The sound came from about fifty yards to his left and somewhat ahead, and then he faintly heard men's voices, at least two men talking. The trees screened them from his sight, but he realized that they too must be trailing the cattle.

He started to cut through the timber toward them, then heard them move off away from the trail, riding downslope toward Leggett's headquarters. Caution touched Will-Joe; he slowed. Maybe these men weren't on the trail of stolen cows; they might be friends of Leggett.

By the time Will-Joe rode clear of the trees and could see the ranch headquarters again, the two men were far below, riding into Leggett's yard. Even from this far away it was easy to identify the lead rider by his tawny buckskin coat and pearl-gray Stetson. It was Sheriff Ulring.

The house door opened now and Leggett came out, pointing a rifle at the two men. Will-Joe sat his horse at the timber's edge, watching the scene tensely. Would Leggett shoot? It wasn't like Ulring to be so slack as to let a cow thief get the drop on him. They were talking now, and Will-Joe saw Leggett gradually lower his rifle.

It was all right then, there'd be no shooting. Leggett was giving up. Will-Joe lifted his reins and put his mount in a quick trot down the slope. Even if he hadn't been the one to lead Ulring to the thief, it wouldn't hurt to put himself (and hence his tribesmen) in Ulring's good graces by showing him where Leggett had hidden the cattle.

Then he saw something he didn't believe. Ulring whipped up his rifle and fired. Leggett's body bounced back against the log wall, then slumped on its face. Shot echoes cascaded from the ridges.

Will-Joe reined in his paint, staring. He saw Ulring's companion wheel his horse, or start to, as the sheriff swung his rifle around. It roared again. The man was wiped out of his saddle and hit the ground in a broken sprawl.

Will-Joe couldn't credit his senses. A man with a sheriff's star had committed cold-blooded murder twice in the space of a few seconds. His thoughts were still hung on that incredible snag, too stunned for any further reaction, when Ulring's stare swung upward to fix on him.

Ulring hesitated perhaps a second before bringing the rifle to his shoulder. Its barrel rose in a swift arc that, Will-Joe saw at once, would end in a bead on him.

Whirling his horse around, he kicked him into a lunging climb of the slope. The paint had nearly reached the trees when his hoofs slipped on an outcrop of crumbling granite, making him scramble wildly for footing. He got his hind legs braced, striking for higher rock with his forehoofs. For one moment before the lunge that would have carried him clear of the crumbling rock, the animal hung sideways as a steady target. In that moment Ulring fired.

The paint reared with a screaming whicker. Hard-hit, all his muscles collapsing in a rubbery shudder, he was falling even as he reared backward. Will-Joe left the saddle with a wiry twist of his body, throwing himself frantically sideways to avoid the sharp-edged outcrop. He slammed the ground on his side and shoulder, then had to roll hard away to escape the horse's plunging fall.

He lay dazed on his belly, dimly aware that the paint was kicking its life away a few yards from him. With a kind of blind urgency he pushed up on his hands and knees, blinking wildly against the watery pain in his eyes. He saw that Ulring was kicking his horse forward and up the slope, roweling the animal with an angry ferocity.

Will-Joe staggered to his feet, surging into a run almost before his feet were fully under him. He scrambled up across the outcrop and headed for the timber. Ulring fired again; Will-Joe heard the bullet spang off the outcrop. He was still dazed, wobbly and half-limping, as he crashed into a fringe of cedar scrub and plunged on into the trees. He heard the hard quick thrum of hoofs terrifyingly close. But then Ulring reached the first undergrowth and was forced almost to a stop.

Panic and a flood of returning awareness jarred Will-Joe's brain back to chill clarity. Dropping into a half crouch now, he glided deeper into the timber, pushing instinctively into the densest thickets and going through them like a snake. He could hear Ulring wallow his horse into the brush, beating at it with his rifle.

That noise ended: there was a lighter, swifter crackling of brush. He knew that Ulring had left his horse and was tackling the timber on foot.

Plunging on, Will-Joe felt a dismal wrench of fear. He couldn't move quietly enough to shake Ulring. The sheriff's ears were wolf-keen; he moved less clumsily through woods than most white men.

He should have had the presence of mind, Will-Joe thought bitterly, to snatch his rifle from its scabbard before taking flight. Now he was unarmed, afoot, pursued by a rifle-armed enemy he'd seen commit two murders.

It occurred to him quite suddenly that he must be giving himself away to Ulring as much by direction as by sound. When had he seen a deer, a fox, a rabbit flee from a predator or a hunting dog in a straight line? They ran a broken course, they zigzagged, they doubled back. It gave a queer abrupt twist to the familiar patterns of his thoughts: the staggering novelty was that *he* was now the hunted, forced to bend all his senses, his faculties, toward escape . . .

A broad clearing opened in the trees ahead. Will-Joe plowed through the last brush and broke into the open and sprinted halfway across it. For the moment he was making no sound but the light running pad of his moccasined feet: he twisted hard in his tracks and cut off at right angles from his line of flight, running noiselessly toward the forest wall a hundred feet away.

A low deadfall lay at the clearing's edge. He stepped over it and dropped behind it, flattening himself hard against the earth. He waited like that, nothing but the narrow deadfall trunk between him and the open clearing. His heartbeats against the loam sounded like thunder in his ears: he had to fight the impulse to leap up and run again. But he couldn't without making a giveaway noise, not through the brush that hemmed this clearing on every side.

He heard Ulring breaking brush in his easy swinging run, his spurs chinking. Now Ulring had reached the clearing, he was inside it, he paused. Not daring to raise his head, not wanting to shiver a leaf, Will-Joe hugged the ground behind his slender concealment. He knew that Ulring had stopped less than thirty yards away, listening, probing the timber with his eyes. Wondering why his quarry had ceased to crackle brush.

Ulring couldn't have paused for more than a few seconds, but to Will-Joe, the bloodbeat hammering in his temples, it seemed an eternity. Then Ulring tramped straight on across the clearing and bulled away into the brush. Its crackling diminished; he was gone.

Will-Joe got slowly to his feet. Reaction grabbed him; he was starting to shake all over. Once the sheriff realized he'd lost the trail, he would (knowing Ulring) swing back and comb this whole area methodically. Moving slowly now and in almost complete silence, Will-Joe slipped into the trees and quartered away into the timber opposite the direction Ulring had gone.

*   *   *

Long before he gave up beating around in the timber, Ulring knew it was hopeless. The kid had gotten clean away. For now, Ulring thought, but I'll find him, by Christ. Yet there was a cold glaze of fear on his mingled fury and bafflement as he headed back for Leggett's.

He'd always gone on the premise that the

simplest plans were the best ones, and this particular idea had seemed foolproof. All the details had dovetailed together (in theory) as beautifully as the joints of a hand-crafted chair. The only real work involved had been driving a jag of Cross T cows across to Leggett's range. It had taken him the better part of last night, and he'd had to herd them by moonlight. The rest had been just a matter of figuring. Anse Burris's morning habit of giving his property a look-over had meant that the theft of the cows would be quickly discovered and reported. It had been a dead-sure cinch that Anse, unable to ride a horse any great distance, wouldn't undertake to trail the stolen cattle himself.

Getting Dennis McAllister to accompany him this morning had been the least of Ulring's worries. Making up a deputy's job that Dennis couldn't afford to turn down had merely meant dropping a casual mention to Bethany; the rest had gone slick as grease. There'd be no reason for anyone to doubt the story he'd give out. That they had trailed the Cross T cattle to Leggett's and found them in the timber above the place. When they'd attempted to arrest Leggett, he'd opened fire; the first shot had hit Dennis and killed him instantly. Leaving Ulring no choice but to gun Leggett down . . .

Coming to the timbered slope above the ranch now, Ulring halted by the brush-broken trail he had made driving the cows here last night. He hunkered down and nudged his

Stetson back on his broad sweaty forehead, staring speculatively at the sign. Sure as hell. In addition to the tracks he and Dennis had made, there were fresh prints of an unshod pony.

He hadn't bothered to examine the tracks closely when he and Dennis were following them. Why bother? He'd known exactly where they led. So he hadn't noticed that at some point—maybe only minutes before he and Dennis had come along—someone else had stumbled on the trail and had been curious enough to follow it up.

'That breed bastard,' Ulring said aloud. Said it as if he were chewing the words up for taste, slowly and venomously.

He hadn't been afraid often, and the quiet dribble of panic threading his guts now had shaken his cocksureness. His tongue tasted brassy. Steady does it, boy. He pressed the flinty edge of his will against the sensation and felt it ebb away.

All right. The kid knew. Who was he going to tell? Suppose he told the whole damn county—would people believe Frank Ulring or a goddam breed brat?

The startling, uneasy thought touched him that he couldn't be altogether sure of the answer. He, Frank Ulring, owned respect, but it wasn't the same as trust. Too much of the respect he'd engendered had been built on fear. It added a tricky, even precarious element to the situation.

Suppose the kid told his story to someone : . . anyone who could get it circulating? Not a jot of support for it beyond the kid's naked word; still it could wreck his plan. People liked to talk. And there was already a degree of amused, inevitable speculation about Frank Ulring's out-of-character kindnesses to the McAllisters. People needn't be partial to a breed's word to see that yes, by God, the sheriff had a clear motive for doing what the kid claimed. While Will-Joe Cantrell hadn't a reason that anyone could see for lying.

So it would go: not a shred of proof, nothing a court of law would take seriously. But the talk was bound to reach Bethany. She wouldn't believe it straight off, of course. Yet it wouldn't matter: once a doubt was seeded, it would grow. She'd never shed her widow's weeds for the man touched by that terrifying suspicion. Before she was even his, Bethany would be lost to him for good . . .

Ulring rose from his haunches and tramped on down the slope, his thoughts seething with the complications that suddenly clotted the sweet-running course he'd set. He halted by the kid's dead horse and appropriated the saddle gun from its scabbard, then continued downslope.

The kid was horseless now, weaponless too . . . that was one piece of luck. Or was it? Young Will-Joe Cantrell had a horse-breaking camp back in the hills—so they said. Probably he'd have other mounts there, and maybe another gun. Ulring had no idea where the camp was located, but more than one citizen of Spurlock must know. Afoot, it would take Cantrell a good spell to get back there . . .

Ulring's brain was ticking coolly as he crossed Leggett's yard. He walked past Dennis's sprawled body without glancing at it, halted by the porch and picked up Leggett's Winchester and fired it off once in the air. That, in case anyone thought to check the weapon later, would be the shot that had killed Dennis . . .

Afterward he roped Leggett's horse out of the brush corral, put on the saddle and slung Leggett's corpse over it. He lashed it tightly in place, then tied Dennis across his mount in like fashion. Mounting then, he rode away from Leggett's, leading the horses with their limp burdens.

He rode easy, not even thinking about the two bodies. All his thoughts had compressed to a hard hot focus on Will-Joe Cantrell.

Slowly he began to grin. Now there was an idea . . . yes sir, it should do the trick nicely. That breed bastard would never get the chance to tell a soul what he had seen at Leggett's. Not with every damned householder in the county ready to shoot him on sight . . .

*   *   *

After Will-Joe's first panic had blunted, he had made a wide circle through the timber and had come up on Leggett's place from the side. Getting hold of a gun and a mount were on his mind. There was a horse in Leggett's corral; there was Leggett's rifle on the porch by his body.

Will-Joe worked carefully through a maze of scrub cedar that bordered the outbuildings on the north side of the headquarters, keeping his eyes on the corral. To reach it, he'd have to make a dash across several hundred feet of open yard.

He was ready to try when he saw sun wink off rifle steel high on the east-facing slope above. Ulring was coming back, just emerging from the timber. Will-Joe stayed where he was, hunkered in the dense scrub. He saw Ulring halt by his dead paint and take the rifle, and proceed down the hill. When he rode out fifteen minutes later, taking along the two bodies, he left no horses or rifle behind.

Will-Joe waited a good ten minutes after the timber had swallowed the lawman, then loped across the yard to the house. He climbed the sagging porch and went inside. The interior of Leggett's shanty was a chaos of dirty junk. He made a quick search for weapons, but found nothing except a rusty .45 with a broken firing pin.

Coming outside again, he paused to look at the sticky drying darkness on the porch planks

63

where Leggett's body had lain, also the scuffed dust of the yard where the man shot off his horse had fallen. He dully wondered who that man was: he hadn't recognized him from a distance. Above all, he wondered with a mounting bewilderment what was behind it. Why, after shooting Leggett in cold blood, had Ulring turned his rifle on his own companion?

Will-Joe went slowly across the yard, studying the ground. He did it out of a horse-trapper's instinct, not expecting to find anything of real significance. Then his gaze found something that made him kneel down for a closer inspection. That hoofprint . . . the two caulks and the shoe built up on the inside. The rider who'd driven off the Cross T cattle had made the same track. But had it been left by Leggett's horse?

A quick suspicion made Will-Joe cross to the corral gate. A glance at the trampled mud of the corral told him that the built-up shoe hadn't been worn by Leggett's animal.

He looked over the yard tracks again, then was sure. It had been Ulring who'd driven off those cattle and hidden them in the timber above Leggett's. But why? To make Leggett out a cow thief? If so, the question only loomed bigger than ever. *Why?*

Will-Joe shivered under the hot sun, feeling a cold despondency in his guts. What could he do . . . and where could he go? Though his camp would no longer be safe, he had to return

64

to it long enough to pick up another horse and a few necessities. Afterward he'd have to stay on the move, making quick break-up camps, never remaining long in one place.

His escape from Ulring had only gained him a little time. Not enough, he bleakly knew. Not enough by a lifetime. For there was always tomorrow. There might be ten or a hundred fear-haunted tomorrows, but in the end Ulring would find him. And never rest till he did.

For Will-Joe Cantrell was the sole witness to a double murder. And the murderer had an edge that was unbeatable: he was the Sheriff of Grafton County.

CHAPTER FIVE

Dusty pillars of afternoon shadow stretched across Spurlock's main street as Ulring rode in, leading two horses with grisly burdens. The day's heat still clung to the town like a sultry blanket; just a few people were stirring outside. These abandoned their errands or their loafing, straightening up, staring, as the sheriff jogged past.

Word should get around fast, he thought, aware that he was a little tired, his muscles layered with tension. But his thoughts had a clear smooth-running grain that pleased him. He had all the particulars of his story figured

65

out and no real worry that any of it might provoke questions he couldn't answer.

He turned into the archway of the livery stable. Claude Warhoon was cleaning out stalls. He stopped, his lantern jaw fell, he almost dropped his long-handled shovel.

'Good God A'mighty! What you got there? Is that Dennis?'

Ulring stiffly dismounted in the runway, then walked up and down beside his horse, working the saddle kinks out, flexing his wrists. He said: 'Want you to take both these bodies over to Doc Bell's . . . have to be an autopsy held. Then see you put the horses up.'

'Yes, sir.'

'After that, round up anyone you can find for a posse . . . spread the word. Tell 'em to meet over at the Pink Lady. I'll be along in a while.'

'Yes, sir. I would sure admire to hear you say what's happened. What do I tell 'em?'

'Tell 'em Sid Leggett and an Injun kid were running off Cross T cows.' Ulring began slowly peeling off his buckskin gauntlets. 'Tell 'em we tracked 'em down and Dennis McAllister got killed in the line of duty. Sid's dead and the kid escaped and I'll need a posse. Get going.'

Claude dropped the shovel and started for the street, his face red with excitement.

'Claude.' The youth pulled up and looked at him, and Ulring said patiently, 'The bodies first, Doc Bell's. The horses—put 'em up. *Then* spread the word.'

Sheepishly, Claude came back, untied the leadropes of the corpse-bearing horses and led them out to the street.

Leaving the stable, Ulring tramped toward the street's south end and the old saddlemaker's home. Though he'd purchased the place for the McAllisters nearly three years ago, Bethany continued to make him regular payments on it, each month doling out a few dollars from her painfully eked savings. Aside from an occasional mild and token objection, he hadn't remonstrated against her insistence on paying: he understood her granite-edged pride in the matter, though she'd be twenty years paying off at this rate.

A smile flicked Ulring's broad mouth. Would have been that long, he corrected himself: Bethany would no longer be saddled with a scapegrace of a husband who gambled away half her slender earnings. Nor would she have a need for wages very soon. The thought came to him with a cool arrogance that he thought was nicely justified.

Turning up the narrow path, he halted at the door of the old saddle shop and raised his hand to knock, removing his hat first and composing his face gravely. Bethany opened the door. She must have come directly from school; she still wore the prim waist and dark skirt that was her working uniform and which she always changed for a gay frock when she got home.

'Frank . . . come in.'

67

He stepped into the *sala*; his spurs rang flintily against the pack-clay floor. Bethany closed the door behind him, her swift glance holding on his face.

'Frank, what is it?'

He bent his head till his chin grooved tight against his throat, then raised his face, feeling only a mild irony at his own histrionics.

'Beth,' he said. 'Lord God.'

'Please!' Her eyes turned darkly intense. 'Tell me what's happened.'

'It's Dennis . . . I took him out with me on a job. We tracked some stolen cows . . . found the thieves. There was gunplay. Dennis caught a bullet.'

'Is he—he's not—'

'He's dead, Beth.'

She was motionless, her tall body straight and Junoesque. Her usually pale complexion had gone almost bloodless. She stood that way for perhaps ten seconds, then made the small, helpless, uncertain gesture of half-turning toward the door. Ulring stopped her gently, a hand on her arm.

'I have to.'

'Don't, Beth.'

'I have to see him. Where is he?'

'No. He's at Doc Bell's . . . but don't go there, Beth. There's no need.'

She pressed a palm to her face, shaking her head. When her hand lowered, her fingers had left flushed stipples in the flesh. 'No,' she

68

whispered. 'I don't want to go. Tell me, Frank . . .'

'Sit down.'

He guided her to the settee. When she was seated, he pulled up an old frame-and-rawhide chair facing her and leaned forward in it, elbows on his knees. 'The blame is really mine, Beth . . . it was all my fault. Christ!'

'What do you mean?'

'Anse Burris came in this morning to report a few cows stolen. A petty steal, maybe a dozen head; I figured some lousy squatter had lifted 'em and we'd get 'em back without much of a row. So I asked Dennis if he wanted to come along. It wouldn't be in his usual line of duty, but . . .'

'Oh yes.' She tightly shut her eyes, then opened them. 'He'd want to go. Any little charge of excitement that might offer itself . . .'

'We caught up with the men. There were two.' Ulring stared at his big hands clasped loosely before him. 'I demanded they surrender. Instead they opened fire. I got one. The other . . . got Dennis. And then he made it clean away.'

'No . . . no, don't blame yourself, Frank.' She gave a slight fierce shake of her head. 'How could you know?' Suddenly she buried her face in her hands. 'Oh—Dennis. Dennis . . .'

He let her weep quietly for a minute, then rose to his feet and touched her shoulder. 'Beth, if there's anything. Anything at all—'

She raised her face, touching her eyes with a wisp of cambric kerchief. He watched her struggle for composure and achieve it. The New England bedrock of her nature left damned little room for self-indulgence: a steel of character that was springy, tough, unsparing of self—rich with compassion toward everyone but Bethany McAllister.

'Those men . . . who were they, Frank?'

Ulring seated himself again, revolving his hat between his hands and eying it solemnly. 'Well, it's not easy to say.'

'Oh . . . didn't you recognize them?'

'Didn't mean that. I knew them all right. The man I shot was Sid Leggett. I brought his body in. But he wasn't the one who killed Dennis.'

'Frank—if you're holding something back from me, don't.'

He gave a slow and heavy nod, lifting his eyes. 'All right then. If you want to know about the one who got away, the one who killed your husband—he was a prize pupil of yours.'

'A—pupil—of *mine*?'

'Will-Joe Cantrell.'

'No.' The pale shock washed back into her face. 'Frank, you're mistaken. You must be!'

'No mistake. It was the Cantrell kid.' He looked at his hat again. 'Dennis and I tracked the Cross T cows into the timber above Leggett's place. Then we rode down to the house. Leggett and the Cantrell kid came out— both toting rifles and acting skittery. That was

70

enough for me. I accused 'em both point-blank. They didn't even try a bluff, just started shooting. The kid got Dennis, I got Leggett, the kid made a run for his horse and broke for the timber. I dropped the horse, but the kid got away in the timber on foot. Searched awhile, but he'd got away clean as a whistle.'

Her hands lay open on her lap. She looked at them a good while, then shook her head very slowly. 'I—I just can't believe it of Will-Joe.'

Ulring rose and paced a slow circle of the floor; he halted facing her. 'I know it isn't easy for you to accept. But how much do you really know about the boy? How much did he ever let you see?'

'I can't believe—to start with—that he's a thief.'

Ulring rubbed his jaw and smiled faintly, sadly. 'Why, Beth, that's the heart of it. Part Indian, isn't he? It's in the blood.'

'Do you truly believe that?'

'I've had experience. Beth, look, Leggett was trash. He was an outcast; so is the kid. They'd figure the same: society owes them something for nothing. So they threw in together for a little cow-lifting.'

'I don't know,' she whispered. Her hands clenched suddenly together. 'Oh, I'm sure it must have happened as you say, Frank. But *Will-Joe*! ... there has to be more behind it, something we don't know—'

A repressed note in her words, her manner,

71

made Ulring feel the full depth of her sick, stunned reaction. Her quiet iron was a deceptive kind of strength: it wouldn't let her give vent to the hysteria that would have relieved another woman. Yet she was more sensitive than most, and the kid had been her favorite of favorites: grafting his lie of Will-Joe's guilt on top of the blow of Dennis's death was nudging her toward a breaking point. Easy on it, he warned himself; give her a little slack.

'Maybe,' he said carefully, 'it happened this way. Kid must have been jittery to start with. He hadn't been mixed up in anything shady before—nothing we know of. He panicked and started shooting, say just at our horses. Never meant to hit Dennis. Anyway he didn't fire again—just cut and ran.'

'Oh . . . Frank, I'm sure that's how it was! He couldn't have meant to . . .'

'Whatever the case was, I have to find him and bring him in. It's my duty.'

'Of course.' She flattened a palm against her temple. 'An eye for an eye . . . isn't that the law you live by, Frank?'

'I don't make the laws, Beth. I don't set the price.'

'But you think it's a fair one.'

Ulring lifted and settled his shoulders. 'Is a life for a life fair?'

'Fair or not—collecting your sort of price ten times over, a hundred times over, won't bring Dennis back.'

'You're too gentle for this world, Beth.'

'Weak is the word, I believe.'

'No. You're tough. Gentle is different.'

'I don't feel tough. Not at all.' She raised her hurt, searching eyes to his. 'Frank . . .'

Ulring picked up his hat and walked to the door, pausing there. 'I'll try to take him alive, Beth. I can't promise any more.'

A grin lurked at the corners of Ulring's mouth as he headed up the street. Boy, he told himself, you missed your calling: you should have gone on the stage. He would see her tomorrow; by then she'd have had a good private cry or two and he could talk with her some more. It wasn't too soon, he thought, for a round of self-congratulations. He'd set the wheels in motion; time and loneliness would do the rest, moving Bethany McAllister steadily toward the closer, always closer comfort that an understanding friend might offer.

Frank Ulring. Friend of the grieving widow. He almost chuckled aloud.

He made his face grim as he tramped up on the porch of the Pink Lady Saloon and shouldered through the batwing doors. Claude had gotten word around fast; a dozen men had already assembled at the bar. They broke off talking and looked expectantly at Ulring as he bellied up. Bert Stang, owner of the place, was behind the bar: a chunky, florid man with pomaded hair and flowered sleeve garters.

'Howdy, Frank. What's all this ruckus

73

Claude's been talking up?'

'In a minute, Bert. Give me a shot of skullbuster.'

Ulring glanced along the line of faces. Most of the men were merchants or clerks; one between-jobs cowpoke was there, and a couple of teamsters. Ulring nodded at them all, called several by name, then looked over his shoulder at the lone customer sitting at a table, the far corner one.

It was old Caspar Bloodgood. Down from the mountains to get his spring shearing and dicker a price for his winter's cache of furs. His presence here could be a stroke of luck . . .

Ulring gave the old man a civil nod. 'Howdy, Bloodgood. How's trapping?'

Bloodgood raised his face from his mug of beer, wiping the foam from his whiskers with a horny forefinger. 'Better'n this stinkin' Spurlock beer o' yourn. I tasted horse pee outshined it.'

Bert Stang folded his massive arms on the bar. 'Old man, you likely have.' He grimaced.

Everyone laughed but Caspar Bloodgood, who didn't give a solitary damn for either compliments or catcalls—or for humanity in general. He came down to Spurlock twice a year to sell his furs or buy his meager needs. Close to seventy now, he was one of the last of the mountain men who'd tramped and trapped this region two generations ago. He stood over six feet in his blackened smoky-soft buckskins—

a dessicated loose-strung bundle of wire and rawhide: you almost expected him to creak when he moved. Even the cowboys and the teamsters, toughly weathered men, seemed pale and almost soft beside him.

Ulring took his whiskey in a swallow; he motioned Bert to set up a round and then began talking. He told them what he'd told Bethany. None had reason to question it; there wasn't a detail that couldn't be verified. All the evidence was there: the cattle trail to Leggett's, the dozen cows hidden in the timber, the kid's dead horse, the bodies of Sid Leggett and Dennis McAllister. Leggett had been friendless and without family; Dennis had claimed no large fund of affection in the community. No one was likely to be particularly interested in how either man had died. Excepting Bethany, who had already accepted the Ulring version.

'One way or another,' Ulring added in a mild voice, 'I'm going to track that breed kid down. Any of you know where his camp is?'

'Sure,' said Cap Merrill, the middle-aged cowpoke. 'I can lead you straight to 'er, Frank. But she's a ways back in the hills and there's a heap of mean country to cross. Anyways he'll know we'd look there first.'

'He's afoot, no gun,' Ulring said. 'I'm gambling he's got some horses and supplies, maybe a spare gun too, back in that camp and will figure it's worth the risk of trying for 'em. He's got to get there on foot from Leggett's,

75

remember. How far, Cap?'

'I'd hazard a good twenty mile as the crow flies. But he ain't no crow. He won't reach his camp before dark.'

'Good. How far to the camp from here?'

'Mebbe fifteen mile. But we ain't crows neither and he's got a long head start. You aim to set out first light, Frank?'

'We've got horses,' Ulring said. 'We've got a couple hours daylight left. Then a full moon to travel by. First light? Hell, Cap, we'll be close onto his camp by then—and be there ahead of him. Lay up for him.'

One of the teamsters rumbled a laugh. 'Count me in. I ain't dusted off a blessed red hide since I sojered at Fort Yuma.'

Bert Stang cocked his brows at Ulring. 'How about that, Frank? You aim to take the breed boy dead?'

'Well,' Ulring said gravely, 'I never could see reading Scripture to any posse of grown men. Particularly when the lad they're after has killed in cold blood. I sure as hell don't advise a man taking any chance with a killer.'

'That's sense,' Bert nodded. 'Kid's part Injun too . . . any man who's fought siwashes knows better'n to fool around. With an Injun you best get in the first shot and make it count.'

Mutters of agreement. Ulring spun his glass between his fingers and listened, half-smiling. Any man here would normally need only the thinnest of excuses to throw down on an

76

Indian. Primed as they were now, they'd need no excuse at all. The Cantrell kid would be dead the instant he crossed any of their sights. He wouldn't live long enough to carry tales . . .

Ulring looked at the old mountain man. 'How about you, Bloodgood? Join the posse?'

Caspar Bloodgood took an unhurried pull at his beer before glancing up. His leathery elfin face was seamed with a mesh of crinkling weather lines, giving it a look that was sly and irascible and puckish. The barber had cropped his long hair off so close to his gaunt skull that his scalp showed pink as a baby's under the sparse white fuzz.

'I cut this Navajo boy's sign a few times. He is tougher'n whangs and smarter'n a whip. You hosses don't bust him straight off, he'll have you all runnin' in circles. Take another Injun to find him. Or me.'

'Seems a fair reason for asking your help,' Ulring said. 'What about it?'

Bloodgood drained his mug and set it down, fingering a few drops off his whiskers. 'How much it worth to you?'

Ulring felt a mixture of surprise and anger. 'Not a damn cent. Matter of a citizen's duty.'

Bloodgood snorted. 'You don't take this citizen on for aye.' He picked up his rifle from the table and stalked noiselessly to the doorway.

Ulring said: 'Know something, old man? As sheriff of this county, I can deputize you into

77

service and not ask your aye, yes or no.'

Bloodgood stopped just short of the doors. He pivoted on a moccasined heel with all the long-muscled grace of a young catamount. When he stopped, his rifle was pointed at the sheriff's belly. A wicked light quivered in his eyes.

'How much you reckon a deputy worth to you, boy?'

Ulring stared at him. 'All right . . . forget it.'

'Smart idee if you did too.'

Bloodgood backed out through the batwings, heeled about and tramped away.

'Independent bastard, that old boy,' said Bert.

Ulring swung back to the bar and reached for the bottle. He poured another drink and swallowed it, feeling it curdle around the hot gut-nettles of his anger. He said thickly: 'The hell with him. All I need is a little moonlight and a few men with bark in their bellies. We start out now, we can finish this before the night's over.'

The big teamster took a slug straight from the bottle and wiped his mouth on a hairy wrist. 'Suits me. You know, though, that old buckskin bastard got hisself a point. They ought to pay bounty on every Injun carcass a man skins out.'

CHAPTER SIX

Will-Joe doubted he'd walked so far in his life as he had through this night and the previous afternoon. He'd been a horseman for so long, using horses in all aspects of his work, that his walking muscles had slumped sadly out of shape. The country between Leggett's ranch and his own camp was bitterly rough; it sloped up and down one ridge after another. Even traveling by moonlight, using trails whenever he could, he found it slow going.

After leaving Leggett's, he'd detoured into the sandy wash where he had first found the tracks. He located the deer he'd cached and hacked some strips from the hindquarters to take along. He might not be able to return to the meat before it spoiled, and there was little food at his camp. He faced a brutal prospect of days, maybe weeks, of hunger and discomfort, of hasty break-up camps that would be dry and fireless, of evading parties of men on the hunt for him.

Tramping slowly through the night while the moon waned west, he wondered what his next move should be. Aside from the obvious one of avoiding capture. He was a loner: his first instinct was to run, to hide, to fight a lonely fight . . . almost anything except seeking help from someone else.

Could he prove his innocence? He didn't see how. Who'd believe that Sheriff Ulring had

79

cold-bloodedly murdered Sid Leggett and another man? Nobody that would do him any good. He thought briefly of Miss Bethany McAllister. But he knew that she had a kind of friendship with Ulring. And suppose she did believe his own story, what could she do?

Frustrations swarmed in his mind. He couldn't just lie low forever: that big blue-eyed wolf of a man wouldn't give up till he was run to ground. Thinking of it, a thin chill washed through him. There were stories about what happened to people—unimportant people—that Ulring went after.

One story in particular. Several years ago when Ulring had been waging his crusade against Navajo thievery, the three Hosteen brothers—members of old Adakhai's band—had run off a few scrawny cows belonging to valley ranchers. Ulring had caught up with them back in the hills. He'd captured two of the brothers; the third, Billy Hosteen, had escaped. Billy had followed at a distance, out of view, as Ulring herded his prisoners toward town. Presently he'd heard shots. A little farther down the trail, he came on his brothers' bodies. Both had been shot through the head, the bodies left for their tribesmen to find.

No mistaking the message. It didn't say merely that Frank Ulring would kill an Indian as casually as he'd swat a fly. It was also an arrogant statement of power, declaring plain as any words that the only justice in Grafton

County was white-man justice. That it made no difference how many Navajos knew how the Hosteen boys had died because if any white man were told, he wouldn't believe it. Or if he did, wouldn't care.

The night heeled over its crest and sank toward dawn. The moonlight lost its raw edges where it limbed rocks and brush; a beige of false dawn blurred their outlines. And still he tramped on, the numb ache in his legs turning to shooting pains. The hard parfleche that soled his moccasins had begun to flap loose. He could hardly feel his feet any more; they had the thick deadness of stumps. He was close to his camp; it was all that kept him going.

The land rimmed into a jagged dark ridge against the pearly fan of dawn. Beyond it, he knew, he would see his camp. Birds were starting up in the trees and rocks; he felt a clear singing rush of relief. But caution tempered it even before he topped the ridge.

Suppose Ulring was waiting for him below? It was possible. If he hadn't known where the camp was, the sheriff could easily find out from someone in town, then get there ahead of Will-Joe. Had he had time enough? Will-Joe wasn't sure . . . a stubborn gambler's instinct told him to go on, take the chance, find out. There were things in that camp he needed, they were his, he meant to claim them. For there'd be no coming back.

He moved downridge at a careful trot,

studying the scene. The dawn light was spreading, freshly defining what had been beige-dull outlines. The camp was valleyed between smooth rises, a little brush and timber fringing their flanks and summits. From where he was, everything seemed quiet, the camp undisturbed since he'd left it yesterday morning. Some rough-broken mustangs confined in a crude corral stamped and whickered as he approached. He was alert: he saw nothing, heard nothing and he walked into camp and lost no time preparing to clear out.

He unwrapped his gear and rifled swiftly through it, taking only what he needed. He had a pistol that he never wore ordinarily; Adakhai had given it to him as a boy. It was at least twenty years old, one of the earliest cartridge-firing models; all the bluing was worn off the frame and barrel, and the butt was reinforced with rawhide patching. He'd always kept it clean and oiled against an emergency he couldn't foresee. He thrust it into his belt, jammed a box of loose shells in his pocket, then made a bedroll of a couple blankets, wrapping them around some jerky and cold biscuits, along with a change of clothes and spare moccasins. As he lacked a saddle, he cut a length from his extra lariat to make a harness for securing it over his shoulder.

For a mount, he singled out the toughest and most manageable mount in his rough catch: a piebald mare with a short-coupled build.

Dabbing a quick loop on her, he led her from the corral and fashioned a hackamore, then slipped lithe as an eel onto her back. After a few half-hearted cavortions to settle her rough edges, she steadied down.

He looked at the other horses. A damned shame, after all the labor of catching and rough-breaking, to leave them for someone else's use or profit. Reining back to the gate, he unlatched it and rode the mare inside, trotting her back and forth, yelling, swinging the double-up remainder of his lariat at the horses' rumps. They milled confusedly toward the gate, then broke out through it and poured off over a saddle that ran between the flanking rises.

Will-Joe followed them, hoorawing them constantly, knowing the half-wild animals would scatter far into the hills. He headed them onto an ungrassed plain that bisected the low hill range. Their hoofs hammered up yellow billows of dust that made him fall back, eyes stinging. As the bitter clouds settled, he sat the mare and watched the mustangs fan away toward the hills and freedom.

He caught a movement. Just a sky-rimmed flicker of movement on one of the hills off west of him. Men were crossing it, coming over its dark backbone, themselves nothing but dark shapes in the sallow dawn hour. They weren't close to him, probably hadn't spotted him as yet, but he was caught in the open: he'd be seen as soon as he moved.

They were moving this way, they would see him anyway when they were almost on him. He hesitated, but not long: this had to be a posse from town. Coming for him. What else would a large bunch of riders be doing out in the pre-dawn ... and heading straight into his camp? Ulring could have given them any kind of story. Whatever it was, it had been enough to bring them out in force for a long night ride.

No time to think about it now. No time to think of anything but escape.

Wheeling the mare in a sudden quarter-circle, Will-Joe kicked her into a run. He headed south by east toward the rugged country that ended at the lower Winnetka basin. The dun earth blurred by; men's faint shouts reached him, not quite swallowed by the mare's thrumming hoofs. The ground began to climb. Ahead, the country was etched like broken saw-teeth on the pallid sky. He felt the mare stumble and slowed with a sharp instinct. Ground contours were still hard to pick out by this light, but their feel was rugged and rock-strewn.

He pushed into a shallow gully and continued to climb, following its dry tortured bed upward. Spired boulders grew around him like monuments; he felt locked in by the rising flanks of rock and cold sweat washed his back and belly. He knew this country, but not in so many details; he could run himself up a blind alley easy as not. With the posse so close, he couldn't be selective about an escape route: he had to feel his way just this blindly and hope for the best . . .

He looked back. For the moment they were lost to view, but within minutes they'd be swarming up the gully. If he were to shake them, it had to be now: he was still cut off from them.

For another fifty yards the gully twisted snakily upward. Then suddenly a canyon mouth yawned to his right. Its breadth seemed to promise a way out; he plunged unhesitatingly into it. He rode as fast as he dared. Hoof echoes clattered off the massive sloping walls with stony fury.

But the canyon didn't widen. Nor did it lift toward higher ground. The walls grew steeper and began to pinch gradually off. Fallaway fragments from the rimrock littered the gorge floor, forcing him to go slower. Panic threaded his guts: it was a bad place to be caught in, and the worst part was his ignorance of what was ahead.

The canyon rims shelved closer together till they nearly met, blocking out the scanty light. He was riding in semi-gloom. Then the walls began suddenly to broaden again; hope surged in him. He must be close to the canyon's end . . .

He was. He came around a bulging angle of wall and he was in a great rock-strewn amphitheater. This was canyon's end: a flat-bottomed bowl circled by high-faced cliffs.

And no trail out. He was boxed here. Trapped.

He'd come too far to turn back. Probably the posse would split apart at the canyon mouth; some would continue up the dry gully, others would follow the canyon. Turning back now, he'd meet them about halfway. And face two options: fight and get shot to pieces. Or surrender and be promptly shot or hanged.

The dawnlight had increased, its stark pearly glow filling the bowl, highlighting the knobby pitted face of the enclosing walls. Enough light, he thought, to scale them by ... if it were possible.

If. He made the decision with no confidence. It was his only choice. The posse must be in the canyon by now, leaving him only minutes to spare and not a second to lose.

Already, as he slipped off the mare's back, he was scanning the cliff for what seemed the easiest line of ascent. He started upward then, driving his toes hard at the talus slant. The first twenty feet weren't impossibly steep, and then he was scaling bare rock, using hands as well as feet. The footing seemed solid; he went up swiftly as a goat.

More than halfway to the rim, he had to slow. The pitch of the cliff was almost perpendicular now, and he chose his holds carefully on its blistered surface. He climbed another sweating yard, then had the sinking realization that he couldn't move past the swell of smoothly outcurving rimrock just above.

A short distance to his left, the rim was deeply split. Maybe the cleft was wide enough to fit his body into; then he could clamber up through it. But the wall was almost sheer at this point. He had to move sideward with infinite care, testing each supporting knob or crevice before he let it take his full weight. The cliff was rotten here, he could feel its crumbling rasp under his moccasin soles, yet he had no choice but to trust it.

Some of it broke away under his groping toes, the fragments booming with a sullen clatter down the cliff face. He curved his fingers into their tenuous holds, feeling needles of pain shoot the length of his arms; blood hammered in his temples. Another four feet . . . he would be inside the split. To reach it, he must grasp a flinty protuberance just this side of it, then maneuver his feet along a ledge about two inches wide till he could swing his body into the cleft.

The knob was just beyond reach of his splayed fingers. He strained sideways with a frantic care, fighting to keep his balance till he could close a hand over it. The bedroll slung from his shoulder was enough weight to dangerously overbalance him on that side. He couldn't make it. He clung sweating to his precarious holds, hesitating. He twisted his body till he could shed the bulky roll. It fell away and bounced down the sheer drop.

He had enough leverage now to grasp the knob. Slowly, very slowly, hugging the wall and not able to look down even if he'd dared, he began to inch his feet along the ribbon of ledge.

Almost at once it cracked under him, scaling off in great rotted sheets—and he was swinging by his hands over a clear drop.

He heard a faint clatter of hoofs from the canyon. Alerted by the sound of falling rock, they were coming fast, they were almost to this end. For an instant all his mind contained was the naked question of whether he would be shot like a fly off the wall or whether, just before that happened, he'd lose his grip and be crushed to a jelly on the canyon floor.

One of his flailing legs toe-hooked blindly into a shallow depression. It lent him just enough support to let him ease the full weight on his arms and sling the other leg around the edge of the rimrock cleft. Securing foothold, he swung his whole body into the ragged break.

The riders thundered into the bowl.

'There he is ... up there! Get him, goddammit!'

Will-Joe was already scrambling up the last few feet. A man fired wildly. The slug caromed off rock yards to his right. Another hit just above his head, showering splinters over him. In seconds, he knew, all the guns would be out, and not all would be wild shots.

He clawed savagely upwards; his hands

88

closed over the rim. A third bullet striking somewhere below whined up and streaked redhot along the flesh of his forearm.

With a supreme effort he heaved his body up and over the rim, rolling away from it. A moment later he flattened under the screaming ricochets as a half-dozen guns opened up simultaneously at the rimrock. He rolled again, scrambling farther off the rim, and fell on his back. His chest was rasped raw, his fingers scratched and bleeding; the ruddy crawl of sunrise pinwheeled crazily in his eyes.

The shooting stopped. He heard Ulring's voice, tight with rage, yelling orders.

He was cut off from below, he was safe. For how long? No longer, he knew, than it would take them to fade back into the canyon and find an easier way to the rim. A few minutes' respite.

He needed it. For at the moment, grabbed by reaction, all he could do was sprawl on his back as he was, spent and shaking.

CHAPTER SEVEN

A mauve blur of dusk had dropped over Spurlock. Frank Ulring's mood was savage as he rode down the main street. He was grimy, sweaty, tired, from twenty-four hours in the saddle with little rest and no sleep. His horse's coat was crusted with dirty yellow froth. Halting at the rail fronting his office, he dismounted like a drugged man. He leaned a moment against his saddle leather, feeling red darts of exhaustion quiver through his muscles. He hadn't put in such a night and day in years; it galled him to realize how out of shape he was.

A week in the saddle would put him back in fettle. For more such days would follow. Maybe many of them. The thought made him swear with venom.

His office window was lighted and the shade pulled. Ducking under the rail, he crossed the porch, opened the door and went in. The sight of Claude Warhoon—dozing in the sheriff's swivel chair with hands folded on his belly, feet crossed on the desk—touched an obscure, furious nerve in Ulring. He slammed the door, bringing Claude wildly out of his chair, his boots crashing on the floor.

'Holy balls! You give me a start there, Frank.'

Ulring came to the desk and slammed his rifle down on it, then peeled off his gauntlets with savage jerking motions. 'Take care of my horse. Then get over to the Chink's and fetch me some grub and a pot of coffee. I want the biggest steak in the place. Half a dozen eggs and some fried spuds. That coffee, it better be black and hot.'

'Yessir—'

Claude was out the door almost before the order was finished. Ulring dropped into his chair and leaned his elbows on it, ducking his head and lacing his fingers together behind his neck. Christ, what a day. Not a goddam mote to show for it but saddle aches and butt blisters. He hadn't counted on how rough the country between here and the Cantrell kid's camp would be. It had slowed the posse by enough to let the kid reach the camp before they did.

It had been such a damned close thing, too—when they had run the kid up that canyon. You'd think nothing alive could scale its box end, but maybe it had only seemed that bad from below. Once he'd achieved the rimrock, at any rate, he'd easily made a complete escape. By the time the posse had worked back downcanyon to a more negotiable means of ascent, the boy was long gone, his trail swiftly fading out in the rocky terrain northeast of the canyon.

They'd found a little blood on the rimrock, but Ulring guessed it had leaked from no more than a scratch. Anyway the kid was without a horse again; he'd been forced to abandon his roll of gear and grub. Ulring had split the posse up, dispatching one man to the kid's camp with orders to lay up there out of sight on the admittedly thin chance that sooner or later Cantrell might return to it. He'd sent others to cover the main trails out of the mountains: if the kid tried to slip out of the county on one trail or another, he'd be held to a snail's crawl afoot. Once he did show himself, mounted men could run him down.

Afterward, judging it likely the kid would look to his Navajo relatives for help, Ulring had ridden alone to old John Thunder's village. He had told Adakhai in unmistakable terms what would happen to any Navajo who gave sanctuary or other aid to Will-Joe Cantrell. If the kid showed up, he was to be seized and tied and delivered to Spurlock. Adakhai had been impressed. Spooked was the word. *Tsi Tsosi* never bluffed, and he knew it.

The threat should chop off any likelihood of interference from that quarter. Would they heed his command to take the kid prisoner? Not likely, Ulring had to admit. They wouldn't cooperate a jot further than necessary; they'd turn the kid away and keep mum. Still Will-Joe Cantrell would be alone, cut off, completely on his own. Probably he wouldn't attempt getting out of the country on foot. Even if he found a hiding place, he couldn't stay in hiding forever; hunger would drive him out to forage. It would be risky to fire off a gun—if he had one—or to build a fire.

So what the hell chance did he have?

Thinking about it, Ulring relaxed a little. He opened a drawer and produced a bottle and glass, and poured a stiff drink. Letting its fluid flame explode through his belly, he felt better. Within a day or so, the whole country would be alert for sign of a murdering half-breed. The Territory's Indian-fighting past was still sharp in memory; people were set to go on a trigger panic at the first hint of an Indian scare. And ready to shoot on sight.

The kid wouldn't live out the week. He'd get no chance to tell his story; no one would believe it if he did. What he knew would die with him.

When Claude brought his meal, Ulring attacked it with a famished concentration, washing mouthfuls down with the black coffee. Afterward, feeling even better, he drifted down to the Pink Lady where some of his posse were wetting down the day's dust.

All were tired and sore-assed; most were taciturn and irritable as well. A soft-bellied lot of counterjumpers, he thought contemptuously: How many would be willing to resume the hunt tomorrow? Only the cowpoke and the two teamsters had weathered the day well, and none of the three were here. One teamster, George Moran, was watching the kid's old camp. Cap Merrill and Tug Baylor, the other teamster, had agreed to go up to the Navajos' plateau, make a cold camp in the hills and spy on Adakhai's people. There was a chance they'd intercept the kid if he showed up, in which case they had orders to shoot on sight.

Ulring had a couple of drinks to settle his supper and then, tiring of the grumbling talk, tramped out. The night was mildly discordant;

tinny guitar sounds from Mextown mingled with the rasping of insects. Chewing a clove, he headed downstreet toward the McAllisters'. In the days to come, he intended to make regular but not-too-frequent calls on the lovely widow. For a long while—against all his impatience— he'd have to continue in the role of sympathetic and understanding friend. It wouldn't be easy, but he had an easy confidence about his long-term prospects.

Also the hardest part was over.

He grinned to himself in the dark as he turned up the pebbled path; he tapped on the door.

Bethany opened it. She wore a full-skirted frock of stiff black taffeta, and Ulring didn't have to feign his admiration. She had never looked so vividly beautiful: the mourning black sharpened every contrast of her creamy skin, her flamelike hair, her jade eyes.

'Evening, Beth.' He was careful to add a small gravity and diffidence to the admiration he let show.

'Come in, Frank.'

She closed the door behind him and led the way into the *sala*. He waited till she had seated herself in a handcarved armchair, then eased his bulk down on the creaking settee, hat in hand. He knew he wasn't too presentable: unwashed and unshaved, red-eyed with exhaustion, his clothes creased with trail grime. And that was how he wanted her to see him:

the good friend and conscientious lawman worn fine in his search for her husband's killer.

'Hope I'm not intruding.'

'Never.' She smiled a little, but dark smudges of strain under her eyes said that she'd put in a trying day. 'Everyone's been so kind . . . people have been in and out all day.'

Offering condolences on her account, he knew—not on Dennis's.

'We didn't find the boy,' he said.

'I know. Mrs Morton told me. Her husband was out with the posse.'

'I suppose'—he gave his tone a wryly impersonal tinge—'you're not altogether unhappy about it.'

'Don't be unfair, Frank.'

'I didn't mean to be.'

'I know.' She bit her lip as if she were trying not to, staring at the thick Navajo blanket that served as parlor carpet. 'It's still so difficult to say how I feel about anything. I guess I'm numb . . . or just confused.'

'No blame to you for that. Anyone's to be blamed, it's me . . . for what happened.'

'Don't.' She quickly raised her eyes. 'Don't say that again, Frank. How could you know what would happen? How could anyone?'

'No one ever does. It's just that . . . a man wants to do something for the best and it turns out like this. I wanted to help Dennis—and you—and now he's dead.'

'Don't think about it any more.'

95

'I only wish I had it to do over.'

A silence ran gently between them. Bethany broke it:

'Wouldn't it be fine if we could turn back the clock on every mistake we commit? All the way back to the beginning?'

Ulring looked at her for a moment. 'You mean with the kid?' He knew she didn't.

'No, I didn't mean Will-Joe.' She folded her hands on her knees and studied them. Or maybe the slim gold band winking on the left one. Then she looked up. 'I still don't believe he's a killer. Not that he didn't kill, I mean. But that he meant to . . .'

'Probably he didn't. I said so, didn't I? But the fact remains, Beth—he was there. He was working with Leggett—and just as guilty of breaking the law.'

'I don't deny that. The facts speak for themselves. But there are other facts, too, in Will-Joe's case.'

'Don't tell me,' he said dryly. 'He's one of the born unfortunates. We all helped push him, all of us. Right?'

'I think so.' She colored faintly. 'That's no excuse, I know. But it's a reason.'

'Reasons aren't excuses?'

'Frank, suppose that Will-Joe Cantrell hadn't been born between two worlds. Suppose he'd had two parents of one race—white or Indian. That he could feel he belonged to one or the other . . . and everything that goes with

96

that knowing. That it might have made all the difference.'

Ulring twirled his hat on one big fist. 'I ever tell you about my father, Beth?'

'You've never mentioned your family. No.'

'He was all the family I ever knew. He came over from Norway before I was born. He'd failed at everything he tried in the old country. His excuse was that when his father died, all that the old man had went by law to the older son—Pa's brother—leaving him nothing. So he came to America. He farmed in Wisconsin. A year after I was born, my ma died. And after he'd lost the farm from drinking and neglect, he made her death the excuse for that.'

Ulring stood, whipping his Stetson against his leg as he paced a slow circle of the room, his shoulders stiffly canted. He didn't have to feign this ancient blister on his soul. 'All the years I grew up, I lived with what he was. From four on, I listened to him cadge drinks, I saw him work at the lowest kind of jobs for drink money. When I was big enough, I had to pick him out of the gutter and drag him home a thousand times. I was Ingvar Ulring's kid. Son of the village drunk. That's how they all knew me. That's how . . .'

He ended it with a laugh. He swung easily around, smiling a little. 'Sorry. But I can't abide excuses. Maybe you see why. If upbringing's any excuse for a kid, I had more than enough to wind up like my old man did. Or worse.'

97

She rose, rustling crisp taffeta; she walked to the window and faced out toward the darkness. 'You're strong, Frank. It makes you expect too much of others.'

'You too,' he said gently. 'Difference is, you expect 'em to be better than they are.'

She turned her head till their eyes met; she forced a little smile. 'And I suppose when they're not, I make excuses for them?'

'Something like that.'

'I wasn't like you, Frank. I had every advantage. I can't help thinking that—and feeling it does make a difference.'

'You were born a worthwhile person, Beth. That's what makes the difference. A worthwhile human being, and a friend.' He shook his head a little, soberly. 'Times like this, I don't know what even the best of friends can say or do that will mean anything ... that will help.'

'So often—you've been a comfort just by being there, Frank.'

Her eyes misted: she dipped her chin down, her shoulders shaking. The signs of an inheld tension and tired grief that couldn't let go of itself. Ulring moved toward her. 'Beth—' He pulled her close and held her till her weeping broke like a storm.

CHAPTER EIGHT

The camp was below him and the four men were talking. They were hunkered in the lee of a rocky spire that partly broke the windy tatters of rain. But wind continued to whip their small fire; rain hissed on the coals. Even in slickers they were wet as rats, chilled and miserable. Not twenty yards above them, Will-Joe was belly-down on a shelving ledge. From here he couldn't see their faces, only the bent shape of their bodies in gleaming slickers and hatbrims troughing the rain off in bright twinkles.

But their voices reached him plain enough.

'That goddam breed is got an edge,' one said. 'You ain't gonna outfigure no Injun on his own ground. It's in the blood.'

'It's his training, that's all,' said a mild-voiced man.

'Bullshit it's training. It's in the blood. That breed got borned with an edge.'

Will-Joe sprawled prone on the rain-beated lid of rock, trying to still his chattering teeth. He'd been working north through the brush when he had spotted the fire. It had seemed worth the trouble to steal up above the men and see if he could glean a useful scrap or two of information. It was still early afternoon; this camp was only a makeshift halt for rest, shelter, warmth. They guzzled black coffee, passed a bottle back and forth and bitched about the weather and everything else that came up for discussion.

None of it told him much. He had made his escape from Ulring's posse two days ago. Since then, the sheriff had been splitting his command into small parties. To Ulring it would seem the likeliest way of nailing his quarry: have his men fan across as much territory as possible at a single time, keeping a constant pressure on Will-Joe.

So far, though, he'd evaded the searchers without much difficulty. He couldn't have said any more than the men below whether it was 'in the blood' or training alone. He was just glad of one thing: that he knew this country as he did the lines of his hand. Some of the posse knew the land too, but not in his way. His was a special kind of knowing, developed by years of living alone, hunting alone, tracking alone. Depending on nothing but his own senses and wits at times when life had boiled down to the hard and barren terms of pure survival.

Below him, they were talking some more.

'Maybe dogs'll do the trick. Didn't Ulring say yestiday he was sending for some?'

'Yeah, to old Will Farley's place. Will is got some hounds. Frank sent Lester Stevens after 'em, but hell, Will's place is down by Conover Junction. Lester be two days getting there and back.'

'Hounds, Christ. They couldn't track a stink bug in piss-poor weather like this.'

'Yeah, three flash storms in two days, now

this goddam drizzle. Ain't no trail left to pick up, you bet.'

'Well, boys, she's bound to let up sometime.'

'Sure, but when? I seen these spring storms go off and on for a week.'

One man ripped out an explosive obscenity; he snapped the dregs of his coffee into the fire. 'Well, damned if I'm gonna ride out any more of it. Like to catch my death as is.'

The others looked at him. 'You quitting?'

'Listen, we-all been beating our asses sore for three days. My old woman cusses me every night I get in, asking when I'm gonna get any work done. I'm wet and half-froze and purely miserable, and I ain't lost no breeds.'

A short silence. Raindrops sputtered in the fire.

'Well, I ain't neither, Tommy,' another man said. 'I ain't shy about saying what McAllister was neither, a cardsharp bastard. That sweet lady he married, though, she done a lot of good for the town. I figure we owe her this.'

'Why the hell you reckon I stuck this long? I feel for Miz McAllister aplenty; she nursed my youngest through the croup last spring. But we ain't giving her back no husband this way. Anyhow I ain't sure that breed didn't do her a favor.'

'That's a hell of a thing to say.'

'It's the goddam truth and you know it.'

Nobody said anything for a while. One man had voiced what all of them had been thinking

101

one way or another. Someone said at last: 'Well, look we might's well knock off. Ain't no sense hanging out any longer in this weather.'

'Yeah. We got a long ride back.'

'Could be the weather'll clear up by tomorrow.'

'Yeah.'

Will-Joe had the feeling it was just talk. These men were about ready to quit the search. It showed in the spiritless, drag-footed way they moved to their horses and mounted. He watched them ride away toward the south. The slow rain fuzzed the outlines of men and horses, and then they were lost in the misting grayness.

Will-Joe climbed to his feet, swaying a little. He had no slicker, no heavy-weave poncho, to turn the rain. He was soaked to the skin and had been for nearly two days. The cold forced itself to his bones with a steady driving ache; his joints were stiff as boards from lying on the wet cold rock. He felt no satisfaction knowing he was still on his feet, still going, after hours of exposure to weather that would have put other men on their backs, raging with fever.

He was in bad enough shape and he knew it.

Soaked and chilled, he hadn't wanted to risk a fire. Hollow-gutted with hunger, he hadn't dared fire a shot at game. On top of that, he was running an increasing fever—his skin was uncomfortably hot in spite of the teeth-rattling chills that wracked him. The slight wound in his right arm, a bullet scratch he'd ordinarily ignore, had gotten infected. The six-inch crease was a livid line, purplish at the edges and fiery to the touch; the flesh of his whole forearm was hot and puffy.

Two days of snaking through rocks and brush, avoiding the scattered bands of possemen, had taken a lot out of him too. He'd stuck to ground that a dog or an Indian would have trouble tracking on, always keeping away from the trails. He'd pictured without much amusement the baffled flounderings of the searchers. He had already guessed that the number of Ulring's wet, tired, disgusted posse was dwindling daily; he knew the mood of the men on who he'd eavesdropped reflected that of the remaining diehards.

None of it, at this point, gave him much comfort.

Until a few hours ago he had been simply keeping on the move, taking time out for brief rests and snatches of sleep. He hadn't held to any particular direction, nor did he have any specific plan. Except that something in him refused to admit that slipping quickly and quietly out of the country was the simplest way out of his dilemma. He wasn't sure what it was. Maybe a rebellious outcry from his father's stubborn Scotch-Irish nature; maybe the deeper thrust of his Indian blood, the love of a land where he'd been born and seasoned toward young manhood.

Either way—he wasn't running anywhere. He'd decided as much after his escape from the box canyon. Keep on the move to avoid capture was his only thought. This in spite of the belly-deep sense of desperation and hopelessness he felt.

A temporary reprieve—if not a sure way out—had suggested itself almost from the first. That was to seek help from his mother's people. He'd rejected the idea for several reasons, There were those among Adakhai's band, friends of his boyhood, who would give him any aid he asked, hide him out, lie for him if need be. The trouble was, it might put them in jeopardy. Sheriff Ulring wouldn't overlook the Navajos in his efforts to head off the fugitive. He had probably gone to them already and issued a pointed warning . . .

Still—Will-Joe couldn't deny that his reluctance to seek Navajo help ran even deeper than a reluctance to put his tribesmen in danger. When he'd left their lodges three years ago, a bitter vow to never return had burned in his throat.

The acid fury his mother had felt against the white man who'd deserted her in pregnancy had never lessened. A burly, brawling trapper, Saul Cantrell had been a light-hearted footloose sort. Even old Adakhai, who had liked the white man enough to make him a blood brother, had warned her against entering into marriage with him. When Saul one day shouldered his rifle and his traps and went whistling his way across the mountains, she had been crushed. For years afterward her disgrace was aggravated by the twitting and teasing of the other women. And all this she had turned in hatred against her half-white whelp; he had felt the edge of her unspoken hate as long as he could remember.

He had been in his teens before his mother's long-stored venom had finally burst in his face with a hot bitter rush of words that could never be taken back, never forgotten. They were brand scars on his brain. Even when, a year after leaving the band, he'd gotten word of his mother's death, he had felt no inclination to return. The former goodness of that life was gone for him. Blurred to wooden and dust-dead memories by his exposure to the white world and the lonely way he'd forged for himself . . .

Early this morning, though, he'd had some sobering second thoughts about seeking out his tribesmen.

He had come sluggishly awake, dizzy and feverish, in the dripping thicket where he'd taken shelter, and found his arm bloated with infection. It needed treatment, and soon. Certain clans, he knew, guarded the secrets of tribal medicine: any member of such a clan would know the herbs, the brews and poultices, that would draw the fever and reduce the swelling.

Striking out north across the high country, Will-Joe had thought he could reach the Navajo village around nightfall. It wasn't far away, but the rough terrain made bitterly rough going for a man on foot, weakened by hunger and sickness.

Now—drenched and shivering—he began tramping north again, his shoulders hunched against the icy drizzle. Maybe it was only a middling cool rain, but he'd dogged it so long through the slashing wet gusts that he felt frozen to the bone. He had read in one of Miss Bethany's books about a torture the Chinese used: a drop of water falling every minute on a man's head till its monotony pounded the brain with madness. He judged that steady rain could probably do the same after awhile . . .

Hours later, he descended into a valley that bisected by a small tributary of the Winnetka. Usually a deep but mild stream, it was fed by the storm to a boiling yellow fury that spilled over its banks. About a mile upstream was a fording where it ran so shallow a rider could cross and hardly wet his mount's fetlocks. But it meant a long detour; he thought it would take too much out of him.

Even at this point he could ordinarily cross the chest-deep current with ease. He remembered that much. And lightheaded with fever, didn't hesitate. Stumbling-tired, his muscles sluggish as syrup, he plunged into the water.

At first he found solid footing. But at knee depth the bank fell away. Then he was floundering in the current, being swept down its roiling millrace. He was helpless as a cork: all he could do was strike out with his hands and fight to keep his head above water.

The clutch of fear lent him energy. He put it all into swimming hard for the north bank. It wasn't over two yards away, but he must have been carried a hundred feet along the muddy current before he was able to paddle within grabbing distance of some willow trailing in the water. Seizing a fistful of the wiry fronds, he began pulling himself hand over hand toward the bank. The surging water fought to keep its grip on his trunk and legs and he fought back. Slowly, inching up the bank, he dragged himself free of the stream's angry pull.

Then he was face down on the ground, his last strength spent. He was battered numb; drowsiness seized him. He wanted to lie where he was and sink into the earth till he was one with it, flesh into soil, bone into rock. It was the madness of near-final exhaustion and he fought this too, rolling onto his side and then up to his haunches. He let his head hang between his knees, resting.

Finally he forced himself back to his feet and slogged doggedly on. It was twilight, or close to it. The drizzle had slacked off. The horizon west to north was a weird saffron band under the lead-gray sky. The land ran in black undulations below it, like a slumbering snake.

The country climbed steadily. It was full-dark as Will-Joe struggled the last few yards to the crest of a vast granite-spined ridge. He was trembling all over, his head swimming, legs rubbery with exhaustion. He had to rest again. He sank down on the stony cap of the bluff, head on his knees. The rain had stopped completely, but a damp wind off the heights hit his fever-hot flesh like icicles.

He wasn't five miles from the plateau where the Navajo village was, but he was almost used up. He needed a warm fire, food, sleep. He wondered if he could flail his tortured body back to the agony of movement.

He could feel his senses slipping away. No . . . he couldn't pass out now. Not this close. It took a concentrated effort to force himself to his feet again. He crossed the ridge summit to begin the long descent of its other side.

He stopped. A ruddy fan of light spilled up from the ridge base. A fire. But whose? It was a watery orange blur in his sick eyes. He squinted, trying to pick out detail. The scene focused a little. It was a well-made camp. He could tell that much. A man was squatting in front of the fire, but the bright backing of flames gave only a nameless silhouette to his head and shoulders.

Faintly the aroma of coffee and bacon swept up along the ridge slant. Will-Joe's young stomach squirmed with a healthy violence.

Fever had partly deadened his hunger pangs; they rushed back. Saliva churned in his mouth.

Was the camper friend or foe? He didn't know. All he was sure of, he was faint with hunger and the man below had food. That was enough. Risk or not, he was going to get some of it . . .

He slipped down the side of the ridge, dropping into a heavy scrub of young spruce. It cut off his view of the camp. He had to feel his way downward, working toward his deep right, keeping the rough location of fire in mind. The ground began to level off; firelight tinged the black brush ahead. He crept forward, his pistol out.

He came to a mass of rock that rimmed one side of the clearing. Making no more sound than a cat would, he thumbed back his pistol's hammer and slid fast around the rock, wanting to surprise the camper.

He was the surprised one: he froze in a half-crouch. Everything was as it had been from above except that the fire flickered over a deserted scene. The man was gone.

Hearing a whisper of sound behind him and to his right, he dived for the ground without even a glance toward the noise. He lit on his side, body doubled so he could let his impetus roll him over once. He did it just that quickly. And flipped up in a squatting position on his heels so that he was facing the spot where he'd heard the sound.

The man chuckled quietly. It was Caspar Bloodgood. He stood in front of the brush that had concealed him. His rifle was leveled on Will-Joe's head.

'You 'most caught me napping, young 'un. You tripped a pebble offen the slope, though. Made a mite o' noise.'

'So did you,' Will-Joe said thinly.

The two eyed each other a moment, wary as foxes. Neither had caught the other: it was a dead stand-off. Will-Joe's gun was up and centered on Bloodgood's chest.

'You want something, boy?'

'Something to eat.'

Bloodgood gave his rusty chuckle and moved his rifle slowly, slowly, till the muzzle pointed offside at the fire. Bacon sizzled in a skillet; a sooty coffeepot bubbled. 'Well, best get at 'er or she'll all burn up on you.'

Will-Joe rose and moved to the fire and crouched beside it, never taking his eyes or his gun off the trapper. He pulled the skillet and pot off the fire to let them cool. Bloodgood catfooted over and squatted down a couple of yards away. He grinned. He still had all his teeth, yellow and sound.

'You don't need to be skittish o' me, boy. I don't run with no tame pack. I hain't after your scalp.'

Will-Joe said nothing. He knew Bloodgood from the occasional encounters any two men might have who plied lonely trades in a solitary stretch of country. He didn't like the man. Never had. He couldn't say why. He judged men as he did the horses he broke, intuitively and unthinkingly. Some had a streak of pure mean, that was all.

He fished a piece of bacon from the skillet with his fingers.

'Bread there.' Bloodgood's fire-flecked glance nudged a canvas sack by the fire.

Will-Joe opened it and found a loaf of stale bannock. He tore off a chunk with his teeth and ate one-handed, keeping the gun on Bloodgood. As he ravenously bolted down the food, he looked over the camp. There was a businesslike disposition of gear, a pile of traps set off by a tight-looking shelter: sapling trunks bent over and lashed crosswise and thatched with interlaced spruce boughs.

He soaked up the last bacon grease with the bannock and finished it off. He didn't see a cup, so he drank the coffee straight from the pot, straining out the grounds with his teeth.

He felt better. The food in his belly behaved as if it meant to stay down; the fire was starting to thaw his cold-stiff limbs. He felt almost human again. And suddenly sleepy.

'They been crowding you, hey, boy? You look like you been up the mountain and down again.'

Bloodgood's face had a primitive hard-boned look in the raw dance of light. Will-Joe studied it, wondering if the trapper were here by mere accident. Sheriff Ulring might enlist the aid of a man as woods-wise as Caspar Bloodgood. No . . . he was too suspicious now. Bloodgood always moved around, never staying at any camp long.

'You know about it.'

'Was in town three days ago.'

'You are not interested in taking me in?'

'Now why'd I do that, boy?'

'Maybe for money.'

Bloodgood whacked his knee. His mouth laughed; the rest of his cold elfin face never twitched a muscle. 'If that ain't a caution, now. You think so, boy, you best keep that gun p'inted.'

'You wanted to dust some 'un, you should o' picked Ulring 'stead o' that sorry dude.'

'Dude?'

'Feller you shot at Leggett's place. Name was McAllister, as I recall. Ulring hired him for deppity.'

'Dennis McAllister?'

Bloodgood grunted.

Will-Joe stared at the fire a while, the flames rippling between his half-shut eyelids. Finally he said: 'Is that what the sheriff told? That I killed Mr McAllister?'

'What'd you reckon he'd tell, boy?'

Will-Joe shrugged. 'Something like that, I suppose. It is a good story.'

'You saying it ain't so?'

'What does it matter what I say?'

Bloodgood scratched his stained whiskers. 'Mebbe naught. Mebbe plenty. If they's a different story, you best tell me it.'

'Why?'

'Right now, boy, you are on the short end for friends. Better start figuring if you want to slip your tail outen the crack it's in, you gonna need a friend.'

'You could be a friend, eh?'

'Might be. Might be. Years back I knowed your pappy, old Saul. He warn't a bad sort, for all you might think. He allus dealt me square. For old time's, now, I could see his boy got dealt square.'

Will-Joe watched his face. It told him nothing. But he couldn't see the harm in telling Caspar Bloodgood what had really happened. As long as he didn't trust the man any other way, how could Bloodgood use the information against him?

He talked for some minutes.

'So Ulring done it hisself.' Bloodgood grimaced. All the sly seams of his face meshed in a genuine animation. 'Set up the whole thing, run them cattle off and all, to murder that sorry dude. Hey? That it, boy?'

'I saw him shoot Mr McAllister. I did not see him take the cattle, but the thief rode his horse. The tracks said so.'

'Ain't that a caution. Why you reckon he done all that?'

'I don't know.'

113

'Boy, that is a fine tight crack your tail's in. I'll poke around some. Can mebbe find out summat.'

'What can you do? There's no proof. Even the tracks of his horse ... the rain has wiped those out.'

'Just lea' me poke around.' Bloodgood pulled at his nose, his eyes fire-bright. 'Lea' me do that. Suppose'n I found out why he wanted McAllister dead ... ain't no telling what might happen.'

Will-Joe got to his feet. Some of the stiffness had left his body and his head felt clearer. Bloodgood grinned.

'Reckon you'd be bound for the Navajo lodges.'

'No,' Will-Joe lied.

'Don't make no mind to me, boy. Only thing, I find out summat, how do I tell you?'

Will-Joe said nothing.

'You don't need to trust me none. I be around these parts any time you hanker to find me.'

Will-Joe nodded. 'Thank you for the food.'

He backed out of the camp, keeping his gun pointed till he was deep in the trees. Then he continued on his way, feeling stronger, hurrying now.

He didn't know what Bloodgood had in mind. Nor did he really hope for anything. He wasn't surprised that Ulring had thrown the blame for McAllister's killing on him.

The real and bitter shock that came with Bloodgood's revelation was realizing that Miss Bethany would believe it was he who'd murdered her husband. An intolerable pain twisted in his chest. She would loathe him—she would hate him.

Somehow he had to see her. To let her know the truth. Even if she didn't believe it, she had to be told what had really happened at Leggett's ranch . . .

CHAPTER NINE

Will-Joe tramped steadily north. The night was moonless, but now he was following trails he knew so well he could almost have felt his way along them blind. Weariness tugged at his heels, but Bloodgood's grub sat warm in his belly, renewing his energies a little. His arm throbbed steadily, occasionally giving a knifelike stab of real pain.

He passed over two more heavily brushed ridges and tackled a final rough ascent to the long plateau of Adakhai's village. The rocks and weeds under his feet gave way to cushiony clumps of bunchgrass. Dying fires spattered the night ahead of him; hogans mounded indistinctly against the purple-blue sky. The village was sleeping. He slowed his steps.

Ulring wouldn't have overlooked the

Navajos. He'd almost certainly paid the plateau a visit by now. Perhaps he'd searched the village—perhaps only issued a pointed warning. Remembering their old fear of the lawman, Will-Joe guessed that many would be reluctant to help him; others would stand by him no matter what.

But none of these would make the decision. That rested in the withered palm of Adakhai himself.

Will-Joe went slowly, ready for anything. Adakhai had always kept an armed sentinel or two patroling the village outskirts by day and night. He had been a war chief in his early years; such precautions were second nature with him. But his war days were in the far past, when the Navajos had been as fierce and battle-blooded as their Apache cousins.

Adakhai had been at Canyon de Chelly when Kit Carson had rounded up the Navajos and sent them to the Corn River bottoms to become peaceful herders and farmers. When the final bitter blow had fallen, the government selling their Corn River lands to the railroad, Adakhai had fled with his band to timber country in the mountainous north. Here, far from the cliffs and mesas of their ancestral home in the Painted Desert, they had made a last stand. But the expected move by the U.S. Army never came; their squatters' rights were never contested. Rooting a hundred or so Indians out of a remote stronghold would have been more trouble than it was worth—so long as whites in the region kicked up no great fuss about their presence. Adakhai had held his people generally in check, avoiding any major trouble. And even small-scale depredations by the band had ceased after Ulring's harsh ultimatum to the old chief . . .

As Will-Joe had expected, the dogs picked him up. About a half-dozen of them filled the night with a fierce commotion. He walked boldly on till a man's sharp voice hailed him:

'*Taahoo nahi nani.*'

It was an order to stand still. Will-Joe did as he was told. He saw a dark shape coming at a trot; starlight frosted the barrel of a rifle.

'*Haaash yinilege?*' demanded the other, and now Will-Joe recognized the voice.

'*Ahalani, anaai,*' he said. 'Greetings, brother. Is that Narbona?'

Billy Hosteen halted in surprise. 'Is that Jahzini?' Caution touched his voice. '*Ha'at ishi?*'

'I want to see Adakhai.'

Billy Hosteen grunted and came toward him till his rifle muzzle was an inch from Will-Joe's belly. 'You were a fool to come.' His tone was curt and cold. '*Tsi Tsosi* has been here.'

'That is no surprise.'

'Is it true? You killed a white-eyes?'

Will-Joe looked down at the rifle, feeling a mingled hurt and irritation. Billy Hosteen had been one of the few Navajos to visit his camp

117

after he had quit the band. They'd always been friendly, but there was no friendliness in this meeing.

'I will talk to Adakhai.'

Billy Hosteen stepped to one side, then motioned with the rifle. 'Walk ahead of me.'

He didn't move. A stubborn anger welled in him. 'I came as a brother. If I am an enemy, there is a better thing to do.'

Billy Hosteen seemed to hesitate a long moment. Then he swung around and headed toward the lodges, and Will-Joe fell in behind him. The dogs were still yapping and baying, and several Navajos had emerged from their dwellings, their voices sleepy and querulous. A dog made a rush at Will-Joe and Billy Hosteen sent him howling away with a well-aimed kick.

Somebody stirred up a fire. The sleepy mutterings died away. The Navajos stared as Will-Joe tramped past them. He knew all the faces. Some had once been friendly, but there was no reading what lay behind any of these. He said a quiet, courteous *'Ahalani'* to each. Several answered.

Billy Hosteen halted by a logs-stacked-up house. A large hogan made of piñon logs, boughs and cedar bark, it showed the white man's influence. It boasted a lot more in room and comfort than the old-style forked-together hogans whose structure the talking God had decreed long ago. Billy scratched on the woven-reed door.

118

Someone was already stirring around inside; the door was pushed open. A girl's face was dimly ovaled. *'Ha'at ishi?'* Her eyes moved to Will-Joe. She pressed a startled hand over her mouth, then quickly turned her head, speaking into the cherry-glowing dimness: *'Natani— Natani!'*

A man came out, stooping beneath the low doorway. He was tall and old; the flesh had melted from his great bones and his shoulders were bent with years. He hugged a blue-and-red *bayeta* blanket around him against the night chill. His face was webbed with furrows of age and weather, like a mask of brown clay baked by endless suns.

'Xoxo naxasi, Natani,' Will-Joe said respectfully: it was the formal greeting reserved for a chief.

Adakhai moved forward. One long step— then he caught himself. *'Ahalani, shiyaazh.'* His voice trembled with feeling. 'Greetings, my son. What do you want?'

'Di bonaxo sinini,' Will-Joe said slowly. 'Of this you have been told.'

Adakhai gave a laborious nod and opened one clenched hand in a vague motion. 'We will speak in my house. Leave us, Narbona.'

Billy Hosteen looked at him, then at Will-Joe; he looked longest at the girl in the doorway. Then he turned on his heel and walked away.

The girl moved aside to let Will-Joe enter. A

119

trench full of banked coals glowed in the center of the dirt floor. She dropped in some sticks and poked the fire to blazing life, coating the interior of the hogan with a vibrant play of light and shadows. The burst of heat gave a pungent edge to the smell of greasy mutton that filled the place.

The girl straightened from her task and turned to look at him. Her hair shimmered like ink in the firelight. She was thin and slight in her blue velvet tunic and voluminous skirts of black wool, but there was something wiry and tough about her. Her face, though, was gentle and shy, her eyes like tar pools against her golden-copper skin.

'*Ahalani*, Rainbow Girl.'

'*Ahalani*, Jahzini.'

Adakhai shuffled to the fire and seated himself with rheumatic difficulty, crossing his bony legs. Will-Joe eased himself down opposite the old man. The outfanning heat washed through him. The moment his quivering muscles relaxed, he felt the vast weariness hit him like a fist.

'*Tsi Tsosi* came to us,' Adakhai said.

'This I know.'

'You bring danger to us, Jahzini. This you know too.'

Anger and dismay ran together in Will-Joe's mind, even though he'd been braced for something of the sort from this man who'd raised him as a son. 'I did not mean to stay long. I came for food. And there is this—'

He rolled up his sleeve and held out the swollen arm. The girl made a little throaty sound and stepped forward as if to see it better. Adakhai gave her a look that stopped her; she sank back on her knees by the fire, but the shiny tarspots of her eyes held on Will-Joe. Adakhai leaned forward, peering at the arm, then raised his eyes.

'*Tsi Tsosi* says you killed a *Belinkana*.'

'He lies. Two Americans are dead, but it was *Tsi Tsosi* himself who killed them.'

Adakhai's eyes glimmered with a faint rising interest. 'Tell me of this.'

Will-Joe began his story, but his words kept trailing away in heavy yawns. He nodded off twice during the telling. Adakhai toyed with the ancient *bizha* dangling by a thong from his belt. It was his personal fetish that Will-Joe had seen many times: made of turquoise because Noholike, god of gambling, had always been successful with turquoise; and even among the wager-loving Navajos, Adakhai had once been notorious for betting on anything and everything. But his gambling days were over, Will-Joe thought: Adakhai no longer took chances.

When Will-Joe had finished, the old man seemed to retreat deeper into his blanket, mumbling, 'You should not have come here. You bring trouble. We do not need trouble; we have had enough.'

'I didn't come to stay. I don't mean to stay long,' Will-Joe tried to keep any feeling that savored of contempt from his voice. 'Who can know?'

'*Tsi Tsosi* has two men in the hills.' Adakhai waved a hand vaguely southward. 'They have a camp there and by day they watch us. They think we do not know of them. The white-eyed fools are like blindworms; they see yet do not see.'

'I came by night. They will not know.'

'Then you must be gone before the sun comes.' Adakhai rocked to and fro, huddling to the fire as if his old bones couldn't absorb enough warmth. 'We will give you food; Rainbow Girl will care for your arm. She knows the medicine secrets of our family. Then you must be gone, Jahzini. Do not come again.'

Will-Joe bit into his lower lip, hesitating—before the man he had once revered above all others—to say his mind. But the thoughts were too strong, and he bit them out like pebbles: 'I wonder if this can be the one I knew. The Adakhai who fought the Apaches, the Mexicans, the Americans in our good days. The Adakhai whose body carries the scars of a grizzly he fought with bare hands. Who taught me that nothing should be feared but fear.'

A hot glaze passed over the old man's black-stone eyes and faded. 'Youth sees nothing but itself,' he muttered. 'Nothing else—not even its own end. I spoke the truth to you, Jahzini.

When a man learns what fear is . . . he fears.'

He rose slowly to his feet, moving like a man bowed with twice his years, and shuffled to his pallet of blankets in the corner. He sat heavily down, his legs crossed, and fumbled up a cork *tusjeh* and took a long pull at it. Rainbow Girl's skirts rustled as she came to Will-Joe's side and knelt. She grasped his arm at the wrist and ran her flat callused palm along the swollen flesh.

'A bullet made this?'

'Yes.'

'How long ago?'

'Three suns.'

She turned her head. *'Natani.'*

'Ehh?' Adakhai's eyes already had a hotly varnished sheen from the raw corn liquor.

'You must not send him away tonight.'

'Ehh? What do you say, girl?'

'This arm is very bad—'

'It's a scratch.'

'It's a scratch that will kill. I'll have to make a good medicine. There are things I'll need . . . I cannot get them till the sun is up. Then— Jahzini must have rest.'

'He cannot stay,' Adakhai singsonged. 'There is great danger for all while he remains.'

'He must stay.' Her voice did not sharpen but a quality entered it that Will-Joe recognized: this girl was, after all, Adakhai's own blood. 'Through another sun at least. He can leave in the next dark.'

'Danger,' muttered Adakhai.

123

'There is always danger. *Tsi Tsosi* is a wolf; he has a wolf's eye. For no reason, not even for this, he might kill us all. Jahzini was as a son to you, *Natani*. You can't send him out to die!'

Will-Joe felt something constrict in his chest like a tight-drawn knot. 'I will not stay,' he said suddenly. And started to rise.

Her hand closed on his shoulder, pressing down with her weight against it, holding him. '*Natani*,' she whispered.

Adakhai took another swig from the *tusjeh*. He held out a shrunken, faltering hand. 'Stay, Jahzini. Now it is I who ask.'

'Think of the people,' Will-Joe said bitterly. 'You were right.'

'For the people, I ask. Not for what we are, Jahzini. For what we were. Stay.'

Will-Joe sat back. Still resting her hand on his shoulder, Rainbow Girl said: 'You must eat now.'

'I am not hungry now.'

'It will pass. Tonight you rest. Sleep well. It will work against the poison. In the morning, I will make the medicine.'

She began preparing a pallet for him by one wall. Will-Joe watched her gratefully, his eyes burning for sleep. Old Adakhai raised his cracked voice in a *hozhoni* song, the songs that made one holy. This one was the War God's song. Will-Joe listened with no feeling of irony and the burn in his eyes was softened by a misty remembering . . .

*　　　*　　　*

For a moment, coming awake, he didn't know where he was. The bent-pole bark-thatched ceiling arched darkly above; roseate dawn stained its smokehole. Morning flooded through the open doorway, touching the simple furnishings of Adakhai's hogan with a muted pearling.

The casual bark of a dog had wakened him. Other sounds washed into his awareness: a guttural music of voices, people going about their daily lives. It was strange, after so long away, to wake up to the familiar village noises. Through the doorway he saw a woman weaving at a frame-mounted blanket; he smelled the strong rendering of the sumac and piñon gum from which dyes were made. And he felt what he'd never expected to feel: the odd, quickening sense of homecoming.

He moved his head slowly, looking about. Rainbow Girl was gone, her pallet empty. A blackened iron pot simmered on coals in the fire trench. Adakhai was wrapped to the neck in his blankets, snoring in thick boozy grunts. Looking at his withered claw clutching the blankets, Will-Joe thought of long ago, a rushing stream and a strong-faced man with patient eyes holding a fishpole for a small boy, the brown hands finely formed and muscular and sensitive. He thought of those hands pointing out the secrets of sky and trail, stringing gut on a flexed bow, chipping minute flakes from a flint that would make an arrowhead, quick to a thousand tasks of strength or skill. Then the pictures faded: there was only a boozy dried husk of a man snoring in his blankets.

Moving his head, arms, legs brought protesting cramps from all of Will-Joe's muscles. He raised his arm and looked at it. Hot and sore, livid and purplish around the troughed wound, but it didn't seem any worse.

He heard the voices of two people approaching the hogan. Rainbow Girl and Billy Hosteen. They stopped near the doorway out of his line of sight and continued to talk, low-voiced. He couldn't make out the words, but Billy's voice was edged with anger. The talk broke off; Billy Hosteen walked into his sight and strode away through the village, stiff-backed. Rainbow Girl ducked through the doorway carrying a basket. Her face was warm-colored; she hardly looked at Will-Joe as she knelt and emptied her basket of the plants, herbs and roots it contained.

After a moment he said: 'What is it with Narbona?'

'It's nothing.'

'Has he tied his pony by your hogan, skinny one?'

She gave him a quick look and did not smile. 'You talk too much.'

126

He watched her quick hands shred roots and leaves and drop them in a copper kettle. She laid paddles of prickly pear with the spines cut away on a flat rock and began mashing them with another rock.

He felt a strange awareness of her. Rainbow Girl was Adakhai's granddaughter, the last living person of his line. She was two years younger than Will-Joe. As a boy, he remembered being embarrassed and proud and annoyed that the skinny brown toddler had chosen to idolize him, tagging everywhere in his steps. Later on they had been playmates, and Rainbow Girl had wrestled and raced and swum like a boy. All too quickly the formality of puberty rituals had split their lives into separate channels, and any common ground, it had seemed, was lost. Rainbow Girl, taking her place with the young women, had been just one more skinny girl. Skinny One, he had called her before and after.

She was still skinny, her movements like the bend and rise of willow wands in a spring wind. She had always moved well. The coppery cameo of her face was finely planed and angled, like a handsome boy's. Yet she wasn't boyish. Stray motions made her heavy clothing yield in places; there were quick limnings of two sharp tiny breasts, of legs that were long and slim and hard-muscled. She was a little taller, hardly more developed, not really different after three years. It should have been disappointing, and oddly it wasn't.

'Narbona and I were friends,' he said. 'It is why I asked.'

She scraped the prickly pear mash into the bowl and began stirring the ingredients together. She didn't answer at once. Finally: 'Narbona waits for me sometimes when I go for water. We talk. There is nothing else.'

'Does he think so?'

'It is nothing to me what he thinks.'

Will-Joe almost smiled. Girls. Here or in Spurlock, they were the same. Playing coquettes, teasing, setting men at jealous odds. Girls everywhere were girls. But Rainbow Girl was only herself. Straightforward and plain-spoken, with no patience for natural caprice.

'There is no man, then.'

'I do not think about such things. *Natani* needs me.'

Will-Joe looked at the old man sodden in his blankets, the empty *tusjeh* upended by his head. 'You and the *toghlepai?*'

'It kills the pain in his belly.'

Her reaction was sharp, and he didn't press the matter. She set the copper kettle on the coals, then fetched a ladle and a pueblo-fashioned bowl and scooped mutton stew from the iron pot into the bowl.

'When you leave,' she said, 'where will you go?'

'I don't know.'

'You cannot hide forever from *Tsi Tsosi*.

He'll never stop looking for you. It is his way.'

'This I know.'

She brought him the bowl of stew and a plate of ash cakes, and Will-Joe sat up, stiffly crossing his legs, and began to eat hungrily. She squatted on her heels by the copper kettle, giving the mixture an occasional stir. People passing the hogan glanced in from time to time; none seemed disturbed by his presence. He guessed that Rainbow Girl had spread a word here and there to prepare them.

'There was a place we had,' she said, 'long ago. Do you remember?'

'What place?'

'The cave where the water runs very fast below. Together we found it, when we were children. We went there often.'

He nodded, remembering. Downstream on the Winnetka tributary were giant bluffs where the stream had carved out a turbulent path. In one they had found the cave, deep and roomy, its mouth almost hidden by a rioting tangle of thickets and vines.

'You can stay there,' Rainbow Girl said. 'I can bring food.'

'No. The white-eyes are watching. They would follow a woman.'

Rainbow Girl didn't comment. She thrust the stirring stick through the kettle bail and lifted it from the fire and set it down beside him. Motioning that he hold out his arm, she dipped a hand in the warm concoction and

129

proceeded to smooth it over the infected area.

'There is a thing I must do,' he said slowly.

'What is that?'

'Miss Bethany thinks that I killed her man.'

'You can do nothing about that.'

'I can tell her the truth.'

Her hand stopped moving on his arm. Her eyes swept his face. 'She will not believe you.'

'Still she will hear it.'

Her hand moved again, slicking the mash with long angry strokes. 'You are a fool. A fool, Jahzini! You have no friends in the white man's town. If you go there, they will kill you.'

'They will not see me come or go. I am no white-eyes.'

Her eyes probed his, hard-bright. 'No, you're only half white-eyes. Maybe it's that half that seeks out a *Belinkana* woman.'

He eyed her with annoyance. 'She is my friend. She was my teacher.'

'Is that where you learned to be a fool?' She applied a last daub of the mash with a slap, making him wince. 'Go! Go to your pasty-faced *Belinkana*. I have wasted a good poultice.'

CHAPTER TEN

Ulring sat on his heels by a small fire and watched his breakfast coffee come to a boil. His thoughts were gritty and wicked.

130

He had spent the night in the lee of a rocky overhang that had given him little shelter from the periodic bursts of wind and rain. The creeping damp had worked through his blankets and clothes. His whole body was stiff this morning, full of wracking cramps, and what sleep he'd managed to get had done nothing for him.

A few days of dismal weather had thinned his posse out till only a few diehards remained. Last night, when they had all pulled together at the rendezvous point, their reports were discouraging. Nothing, not a trace. They were grumbling and raw-tempered, and they had all gone home to dry beds and hot meals. Ulring alone had stayed out, making his camp in a narrow swale between two timbered ridges.

He looked out past the overhang at the hazy sky. A few glowing sunslits cut through the overcast, peppering the ground with pale flecks. The rain had stopped, but that didn't mean anything. It had gusted off and on all day yesterday. The sky looked anything but promising. Wondering if any of the diehards would show up to resume the hunt, he swore feelingly.

Let them quit. Let all the bastards quit.

He scraped a palm over his stubbled jaw. He was jittery and unrested. The strain was wearing at him in a way he had never experienced. What the hell ... nobody had questioned the story he'd told so matter-offactly at the inquest for which he'd taken time out yesterday. The deceased, Leggett and McAllister, couldn't contradict it. Only that damned kid could.

But where in hell was he?

Ulring poked at the burning pine knots with a stick. Something would break soon. It had to. He was only spooking himself thinking about it.

Close by, something gave a sharp snap. A twig or a branch breaking.

Ulring dropped the stick and in the same motion was wheeling around and up off his haunches, his pistol out.

'Best handle that iron light, sonny. I busted a twig a-purpose.'

'Where are you?' He knew the voice then. '... Bloodgood?'

'Right where you are looking, bucko. Watch sharp.'

Ulring saw nothing but a shadow-seamed wall of aspen foliage. There was a scanty rustle of leaves; Caspar Bloodgood stepped into view. He moved over and squatted down facing the sheriff. His horny fingers held his rifle lightly across his knees and he paid no attention to Ulring's gun.

'Getting the spooks, hey, sonny? Don't blame you none.'

Ulring studied him narrowly. 'What the hell do you want?'

'Gimme a cup o' that java and I be telling you.'

'There's no cup.'

Ulring moved the pan off the fire. His words were mild; he made a swift adjustment in his thoughts. The old mountain man wasn't here for coffee or to pass idle gibes. His sudden appearance had a reason behind it.

'I been a-watching.' Bloodgood gave a contemptuous clack of his tongue. 'That kid is got all you billy-goats chasing your tails.'

'It bother you?'

'Naw. It don't bother me, sonny. I would hazard, though, it has lit one hellsmear of a fire under your pants.'

Ulring's guts tightened. Was the old bastard just being fatuous? He couldn't know anything . . . or could he?

'Maybe,' he said softly, 'you've seen the kid . . . eh?'

Bloodgood's eyes twinkled with frosty blue lights. 'Maybe I even talked to him some. Start thinking about that oncet.'

'I'm thinking about it.'

Ulring moved the pistol a fraction of an inch, enough to let Bloodgood sight square down the muzzle. The old man didn't bat an eye.

'Go ahead, sonny. Let her off. Could crowd your luck, though . . . right after Leggett and that dude fella. Man could run hisself clean out o' likely sounding stories.'

'You're saying a whole hell of a lot for a man who hasn't really said a damned thing.'

'You savvy this coon's medicine straight

enough, boy. I know it, you know it.'

'Say I do,' Ulring said. 'You're riding your luck on a damned thin edge, old man.'

'Like hell. You ain't letting no gun off in my face. Reason you ain't, there's more on your mind'n hair and hat. There's questions.'

'And I want answers for them.' Deliberately Ulring cocked the pistol. 'Or I'll let it off. Right in your face. You can believe it.'

'Could, but I don't.' A leathery chuckle tucked Bloodgood's cheeks. 'Take more'n that, boy. A heap more.'

Ulring let the gun carefully off-cock and lowered it to his thigh. 'All right,' he said calmly. 'How much?'

'Five hunnerd dollar.'

Ulring didn't reply for a moment. Then: 'I'll have to think about that.'

'You don't got no time for thinking, sonny. Spit 'er out now.'

'Old man, I haven't one damned inkling yet what you really know. Or what it might be worth to me.'

Bloodgood reached for the pan of coffee and tilted it to his mouth. He drank off half the scalding brew and set the pan down, his eyes sleepy and sly. 'Could be worth your scalp iffen the kid's story is straight.'

Ulring leaned forward. 'All right, you saw him. Talked to him. What are you selling?'

'Mebbe the wherefore of how you c'n get him dead to rights.'

134

Ulring rubbed his chin. Did Bloodgood really know something useful? Or was he just sparring words, hoping for some confirmation from Ulring's own lips of what the kid had told him? Again ... what did it matter? For in Bloodgood's hands, whether he knew or merely suspected the truth, that story could be a weapon. A lever for blackmail. That makes two to deal with, Ulring thought coldly. Two of them now. All right, but one thing at a time. Find out what he knows about the kid. If anything.

'You know where he is?'

'Mebbe, I said. What about it? Worth the price if I steer you right?'

'If, yes. Where?'

'I suspicion he was headed for the Navajos when he run onto my camp. That was last night jist south o' their town. He looked poorly and he favored one arm some. Reckon he was needing help.'

And he could have slipped into the village by night without being spotted by Cap and Tug, Ulring thought. He started a movement to rise, and instantly Bloodgood's rifle was covering him.

'Don't be a fool. You'll get your money.'

'Ain't afeared I won't. Less'n some sheriff gets allowing to hisself how ole Caspar knows a jag too much for his health. Hey?'

'I'll keep my part if I find you've kept yours. That's all you have to worry about.'

135

'Worry about my skin too.' Bloodgood chuckled in his whiskers. 'You already busted two men clean out o' this life, sonny. Are primed to bust another. Wherefores of it don't concern me none. Just this child don't hanker to be number four plew in your cache. Means to keep his skin and collect breed bounty too. Foller me?'

Ulring shrugged. 'It's any way you want it.'

'I be around to collect. In my own time. Watch sharp.'

Bloodgood got to his feet and backed off toward the trees. He melted into them without a sound. And then he was gone . . .

Ulring threw his gear together in a hurry. As he saddled his horse, he remembered (with a twinge of irony) his harsh warning to Adakhai not to give Will-Joe Cantrell sanctuary. Maybe blood was thicker than fear. He hoped so. Mounting, he put his sorrel at a swift gait toward the high trails north.

Bloodgood. As he rode, his thoughts narrowed hard on the mountain man. Knowing only what young Cantrell had told him, Bloodgood was as dangerous as the kid. He'd recognize that Will-Joe's story, even unsupported by proof, could do irreparable damage to Ulring once it gained currency. The five hundred dollars he'd demanded for a scrap of information was a gnat-bite compared to the extortion that would probably follow.

He'll bleed me dry, Ulring thought with

conviction. That's if I let him . . .

*   *   *

He had told Cap Merrill and Tug Baylor to
make their camp high in the timber south of
the village. As he crossed an open meadow
coming up the long ridge toward its timbered
crest, Cap appeared at the edge of the trees
and waved him on.

Ulring reined up beside him. 'Howdy, Cap.
Who's on lookout?'

'I was. Heard your horse coming so I circled
over here for a look. Tug's back in camp . . .
this way.'

Ulring followed him through the thick scrub
timber to a small glade where they had built a
half-shelter of pine boughs. Big Tug Baylor was
squatted on his heels in front of it, scowling at
a stick he was whittling on.

'Tug.'

Baylor growled something and didn't look
up. Ulring dismounted and swept the clearing
with a glance. He saw the ashes of a dead fire.
A thin anger hardened his voice.

'Thought I told you fellows. No fire.'

'We only built the one,' Cap said. 'That was
last night between rains.'

'I don't give a good goddam when you built
it. Smoke carries. Injuns can pick up the smell
even when they can't see it.'

Baylor drove his knife into the earth and

137

stood up, folding his hairy arms. A cold cigar stub was clamped between his teeth and he talked without unclenching them.

'Lissen,' he said ominously. 'We been up on this goddam hunk o' rock three days. Eating cold grub, sleeping in wet blankets, getting ate up by bugs. Whilst you and them other bastards been cozying your asses back in town ever' night. We didn't even build no fire to keep warm. Just to heat some grub for a change. So don't read us no goddam scripture about how we do or don't.'

'Tug says it for me, Frank,' Cap said quietly. 'Job's a job, that's why we stuck. We ain't neither of us daisies and we sure-hell don't smell like 'em. But it's a bitch of a stand to keep a man on three days running. You want to hard-mouth us into the bargain, you can get yourself a couple other buckoes.'

Ulring eyed the two men carefully. They were dirty, unshaved, grubby as hell, and he could see their tempers were rubbed considerably finer than his. He took off his hat, scratched his head and made his grin sheepish.

'Boys,' he said mildly, 'you're right. Man doesn't think sometimes. I'd never get any of those lard-bellied counter-jumpers from town to oblige me the way you two have.'

'Just so you know it,' Baylor growled.

'Matter of fact, just about all of 'em quit on me. And right now I need a couple men. On a hunch, is all. But it crossed my mind the kid

138

could have slipped into that village after dark.'

Cap and Baylor exchanged glances, and then Cap said slowly, 'Been one of us on lookout all the time. Nights too, 'cept when the rain come down hard. Anyways, I was on watch last night, and there was a sort of ruckus around before midnight.'

'What was it?'

'Hell, it was blacker'n a bat's balls down there. All I could tell, some dogs got het up and barked their heads off. Didn't last more'n a minute and they got hushed up.'

'I'll make you a bet,' Ulring said softly.

'Could of been 'most anything, Frank.'

'I feel lucky today,' Ulring smiled. 'You see anything out of the way this morning?'

'Nary thing. You want to come look?'

The three of them worked through the timber to a rocky spur that overlooked the plateau. The cluster of hogans looked peaceful enough in the colorless wash of sunlight. People were moving about their business.

'Tell you what,' Ulring said. 'I'm going to follow my hunch. If it pans up bad rock, no harm done. Here's what we'll do . . .'

Ulring approached the village riding slowly, keeping to the open. On the flat ground just south of the hogans, some boys were playing a game of *nanzah*, running after each other with hoops. They saw the rider coming and stopped. Then they scattered like quail. Ulring grinned: he was recognized.

139

He rode as far as the first hogans, halted his horse and stepped to the ground. The Navajos had left off whatever they were doing and were just watching him. The wind whipped his hat, and he idly removed it and ran a hand through the yellow hair that he knew was like a badge of fear to these people.

Old Adakhai, summoned by one of the women, came striding across the compound, his faded blanket flapping around his gaunt shanks. His wrinkled face seemed turned in on itself as if he did not want his thoughts to show, but there was nothing unusual in that.

'What does *Tsi Tsosi* want?'

'Just the kid, Grandpa. That's all I want.'

Adakhai had spoken in Navajo; he answered in English. And swung a 90-degree-angle glance slowly around him, taking in all that he could see of the village and ready for just about anything. If they tried to slip the kid out, it wouldn't be right past him, but you couldn't tell what kind of a diversion they might try.

'*Tsi Tsosi* makes riddles.'

'No. I make promise, Grandpa. If the kid is here, you give him up now. I'll take it you were holding him for me and we will let it go at that.'

'Maybe he is not here.'

'Don't get smart-ass.' Ulring stared at him a moment. 'If he's not here, I'd reckon you know about where he is.'

'Why should we know this?'

'You're his people. He'd come to you. If you

140

were scared to keep him here, there's places you could hide him. Now you want to understand me, old man.' He held a palm flat up and tapped it emphatically with his other forefinger. 'If you lie to me now and I find out you did, I will be coming back with a lot of white men. And what happens will be like nothing you ever saw.'

*　　　*　　　*

Rainbow Girl had seen the sheriff coming when he was only halfway across the bare flats south of the village. She was walking toward the spring with a waterbag; she stopped and shaded her eyes. She could not yet be sure who it was, but she made a guess. She waited, slim body braced, wind toiling with her skirts, till she could make out how the man sat his horse. That straight-backed arrogance—she could not be mistaken.

She turned and headed back toward her grandfather's hogan. Her heart was pounding and she tried not to seem in a hurry. Surely those sky-pale eyes of *Tsi Tsosi* could see very far. When she was deep inside the scatter of hogans, cut off from the open, she began to run. She reached Adakhai's lodge.

Will-Joe was sitting up on his sheepskin pallet, holding his hurt arm straight out before him, opening and closing his hand as if trying his strength. The arm was bulky with poultice and wrappings. His glance slanted against her face.

'Yellow Hair. He is coming.'

He scrambled to his feet. Then settled his shoulders and rubbed a fist across his chin, as if ashamed that he'd let her glimpse his reaction.

'From the south?'

'Yes.'

'Then I will have to go out another way.'

'Yes, but it is too open around the lodges. If he sees you, he will ride you down.'

He did not seem to listen. She saw the hard line of his jaw and a brittle light in his eyes. Bending now, he picked up his pistol from the blankets and rammed it through his belt.

'I am tired of running. He is alone?'

She slipped the waterbag off her shoulder and let it drop. She looked at him in the yellow gloom. 'Don't be a fool, Jahzini. He can kill you. He is *Tsi Tsosi.*'

'He has no medicine to turn bullets. He can die too.'

'And what will that answer for you?'

He said nothing, but she saw the tension run out of him, an almost imperceptible slacking of weight against his heels, and knew his mad moment was past. Now he would listen.

'Wait,' she said. And went to the back-drawn door and looked out. She saw Adakhai, who had been gossiping with some elderly friends, crossing the village to intercept *Tsi Tsosi.*

She turned back to Will-Joe.

'*Natani* is going to meet him. They will talk, but *Natani* will not hold him long.'

'Then I go now.'

She saw him hesitate, and said: 'What is it?'

'Maybe,' he said slowly, 'it is a trap. Maybe there are others watching . . . waiting.'

'A trap. How can this be? How could he know you are here?'

'I think there's one who told him.'

'Do you think one of the *Diné*, the People, would do that?'

He shook his head, his eyes narrowing. 'I think it was another.'

He started for the doorway and she stopped him, flattening her palm against his chest. 'If it is a trap, you will have a better chance on a horse.'

'Tell me where a horse is.'

'Wait, Jahzini. I will bring the horse here. Do not come out of the hogan till I bring him.'

'But—then you—'

'No. They would shoot you, not me.'

Before he could say more, she took a swift initiative, whirling around and ducking out the door. In another moment, she knew, he would have gone out first. Now he could only wait.

She passed between the hogans at a quick walk and came out of the village on its eastern side. Then she was descending a shallow and deep-grassed swale where several ponies were ground-tethered. She slowed as she went casually over to the ponies, moving only her eyes, not her head, as she scanned a line of scrub trees a hundred yards beyond the swale.

If anyone were to steal up from this side, those trees would be good cover. There was mostly open ground beyond the perimeter of the village, but the few scattered mottes of trees or brush would hide an enemy's approach and supply places to lie in wait. Just a few, two or three men, could cover all the open terrain. And catch anyone trying to cross it no matter how he angled away from the village.

Jahzini would stand no chance at all on foot. And perhaps only a little better on horseback . . .

She stopped close to a blaze-faced pinto. He extended his head and nose against her sleeve. He belonged to her grandfather and was something of a pet; often she fed him bits of carrot and rubbed his muzzle. His chest was powerful, his legs long and rangy. He should add a good edge to Jahzini's chances.

She bent, untied the leather rope and straightened up and around. Her glance ran across the trees.

For just an instant she saw the man. A quick dark form moving at a crouch from one tree to the next as he worked in closer. Then he was invisible again.

Rainbow Girl spoke to the horse. She tugged gently at the rope to start him moving. She walked slowly back toward the hogans. Her heartbeats filled her ears like a thunder of death drums.

The man would wonder about the horse. She was in clear view should he decide to shoot. She ached with the temptation to look backward, but resisted it. What was he doing now? Raising his rifle to take aim? Or hesitating, undecided? All the stories of white atrocities that branded her memory swarmed through her brain. The *Belinkana!* They were men capable of killing women ... children ... anybody at all.

She did not feel safe even when several lodges were between her and the man. And then she hurried. Jahzini emerged from Adakhai's hogan as she reached it. He took the long halter from her hand and knotted it swiftly around the pinto's jaw.

'I saw a man,' she said. 'He is in the trees. Waiting. Maybe there are more.'

A long-muscled twist of his body vaulted Jahzini onto the pinto's back. He looked down at her, then bent over a little. And touched her face.

'*Ah-sheh heh,*' he said.

He wheeled the pinto, heels drumming its flanks. The animal streaked away between the lodges in a south-easterly run. Rainbow Girl took a few steps after him, then stopped, hands clenched at her sides.

A man shouted. *Tsi Tsosi.* He was coming from the other end of the village at a run. But Jahzini was already cut off from him. When

145

Yellow Hair pulled to a raging stop, he wasn't six yards from her. His hands were fisted around a big buffalo rifle, and now his glance moved to her. His face was livid.

Dimly Rainbow Girl was aware of her grandfather hobbling toward him. But she looked only at *Tsi Tsosi*: unafraid now, eyes locking his in a black fury. *Nayenezvani!* Let the god of the four lightnings strike him down!

Shots. Jahzini had run into someone. And quite suddenly he was racing into view again, turned back by the enemy's fire. Hanging like a burr on the pinto's off side, his leg cocked over its back, using the animal as a shield.

Jahzini. She tried to scream but only a whisper clawed up from her throat.

He was coming almost on a beeline toward *Tsi Tsosi*. With his face half-turned against the pinto's neck, he didn't immediately see the white man. And then he did. He yelled into the pinto's ear, at the same time using his knee savagely. Veering the animal hard to his right. Cutting away almost at a right angle between the hogans.

Ulring swung the rifle to his shoulder, the blued barrel moving, following intently as Jahzini crossed behind the lodges. Waiting the moment he would clear of them. Sighting in for the instant he would make a plain target.

Rainbow Girl was moving before the thought had completely formed. She reached *Tsi Tsosi*, she hit out blindly at his arm and rifle.

146

Felt her hand strike metal and the savage jar of it clear to her shoulder as the big gun went off.

Her ears filled with a roaring cascade of sound.

Ulring swore as he brushed her aside. His hand rammed into his pocket; a brass-cased shell winked in his fingers. He slammed open the breech of his rifle, frantically reloading.

Already Jahzini was past the last hogans, the pinto running all out and Jahzini flattened to his withers. He crashed the animal into a stand of aspen. And he was gone, out of sight, safe and running.

Slowly Ulring lowered the rifle. He turned just as slowly. She saw his right hand drop from the weapon, lift, and then swing back and forward. Beyond the blur of his hand she saw his face, the teeth drawn back wolflike. The meaty palm came against her face like a club.

It was a blow, not a slap. The force of it knocked her sprawling. She rolled on her face in the dust, salty blinding in her eyes.

She pushed up on her hands, blinking her eyes clear. *Tsi Tsosi* was running for his horse and she thought *too late, too late*. The words sang in her mind.

Old Adakhai stood looking at her. She rose to her feet and a trembling ran through her. His eyes were like flame. She passed her palm over the warm blood running from her broken lip and met those terrible eyes defiantly.

Then his head turned and it was *Tsi Tsosi*,

mounted now and flailing his horse to a run, that his glance followed. The jaggedness in his look had not been for her.

'Once,' he said softly, 'and it was not so long ago, if a man did that to you, I would have killed him.'

CHAPTER ELEVEN

Bethany stood by the big corral back of the livery barn and watched the white colt. He was champing restlessly; he put up his head in the dimming twilight and snorted and pushed back and forth among the other horses.

'You beauty,' she said. 'Have you been exercised every day? Has he, Claude?'

'Every day, ma'am, sure enough.' Claude Warhoon leaned his crossed arms on a corral pole, a straw bobbing in his lips. 'The boys from your school, mostly three-four at a time, been coming to walk him. When they ain't, I seen to it.'

'Thank you, Claude.'

She watched the colt awhile longer, her nerves twitching with sympathy. How much he wanted to be free, running the wild range he had known. And how well, in her present frame of mind, she understood that feeling. Lately she'd been oppressed by a sense of everything closing in on her: the halters of her various responsibilities, the pressures of her false mourning. How good it would be to shed it all and run free as the wind!

Yet she knew from where the urge stemmed. From the surge of almost guilty relief after her first intense depression following her husband's death. And ironically, Dennis, who had really known her so little, would have understood this once—perhaps sympathized. Dennis had always given way to all impulses and enthusiasms that seized his fancy. Any gamble (and gambling in general) had gratified his nature; so had she, for a while. Bethany herself was dissatisfied with quiet ruts, drawn by worldly excitements. A tendency which had first drawn her to Dennis. But she'd come to a bitter comprehension of the gulf between his surface feelings and her own need—guided by the stern lines of a bluestocking conscience—to plunge herself into the demands and challenges of community work.

Too, she had always hated failure. She could tolerate it in others, never in herself. Her failed marriage had oppressed her. And she was too honest not to admit that part of her present wish to get away from everything welled from a brooding sense of having failed with young Will-Joe Cantrell.

She had placed such hopes in him. He had learned to read and spell better than most frontier-raised whites. He could write a fair hand and cipher in his head well enough to circumvent the trickiest horse dealer. He knew about Bunker Hill and Gettysburg and (thanks to her) could handle a knife and fork with any gentlefolk. ('When,' he had asked her ironically, 'do you think I will be invited to eat with white gentry?')

Yet he had disappointed her. His apparent ambition had impressed her. She had hoped he would return to his people and use his learning to better their lives. But horse-catching had proved the crest of his aspirations. Now he had stolen, he had killed . . . in the best style of the alien culture with which she'd imbued him. And Bethany felt obscurely to blame.

The day had been unseasonably warm. Even now, with twilight fading, the heat pushed down the stillness with the weight of a huge dead hand. The in-pressing dusk was like hot gray wool. Bethany took off her wide-brimmed straw hat and fanned herself.

'My, it's been a scorcher, hasn't it? When do you think the sheriff will be back, Claude?'

'No telling that, ma'am. He ain't showed up in town for three days. Cap Merrill come in for supplies today and he says Frank is been up at his and Baylor's camp a couple times.'

'Well, I'd heard that they had almost caught Will-Joe there . . . but surely Frank doesn't believe that the boy will try to return to his people now?'

'Ain't really no way of saying, is there, ma'am? Frank ain't taking no chances, Cap

150

says. Says he ast him and Baylor to stay on watch up there awhile yet. Course now the Injuns know they are watching, but Frank figures it might make 'em think twicet about helping the kid again.'

'I see.' Bethany touched her temples with her handkerchief. 'I understand there was a girl who helped Will-Joe to escape.'

'Yes'm, some kin to old John Thunder.'

'Rainbow Girl, that would be.'

'Anyways Frank had the kid dead in his sights and she spoilt his aim. Frank was madder'n a switched cat. Later he give old John vow that when he is got more time, he will run his whole damn bunch outen the country.'

'Well, he was angry, of course. I'm sure that when he calms down . . .'

'No'm,' Claude said flatly. 'He don't backwater on no promise like that, Frank don't. Anyways he purely hates Injuns. That first day we was out after the kid, he give the boys plain-out orders. Shoot to kill, he says. Even if he makes like he is giving up, don't take no chances.'

Shock poured through Bethany like a cold wind. She stared at him. 'Oh, really now, Claude, you're exaggerating . . .'

'I am not, by God, I was right there. He said it twicet to make sure we all got it. I heard him, ma'am.'

'Are you sure you didn't misunderstand him?'

151

'Ma'am, when Frank Ulring says somewhat, they ain't hardly no way a body can take him amiss.' Claude snapped his galluses with his thumbs. 'You'd a been there and seen how he was pushing us all, you'd blame well believe it. Frank is bound and determined he will get that kid. He don't care how, neither, long as it's dead.'

'I see . . . well, you have work in the stable, haven't you? I sha'n't keep you from it any longer.'

'Been a pleasure, Miss Bethany.'

'Good night, Claude.'

'Night, ma'am.'

Bethany headed homeward. She walked slowly, her chin bent, her steps scuffing up little puffs of dust. She felt faintly sick, still numb with a residue of shock. Shock—yet not genuine surprise. Why was that? Because she had always known, or sensed beyond those bits of mere hearsay it was so easy to discount, that Frank Ulring could be hard-steel ruthless?

Not that she'd ever deceived herself that such gentleness as he'd shown her was really typical of the man. Nor had he ever taken particular pains to conceal the rough-shod side of his nature. She supposed that she'd always been inclined to dismiss it as one more facet of his touchy pride. God knew he was touchy. Early in their relationship, she had made the mistake of expressing amazement at his wide knowledge of the classics, he had taken a harsh offense that had given her a glimpse beneath his ordinary pleasantry. And the glimpse had frightened her.

That Frank could be ruthless she didn't doubt. But the man of savagely cold-blooded purpose that Claude had described? You cannot judge in haste, she told herself. The truth is never that simple. There's so much more than appears on any surface. Frank had promised her that he would do his best to take Will-Joe Cantrell alive. That was what really hurt, she argued. It was less likely that he had consciously broken his word than that he had simply ignored it for reasons of his own. That was like Frank; he was that kind of man. Arrogant, overbearing, full of monolithic prejudices that had often stung her sensibilities. She had learned to accept them, and it was just a step to admitting other imperfections in his character. Why should it be surprising that such a man's faults towered as tall as his virtues? If you accepted the best of a man in friendship, weren't you obliged to accept all of him?

Bethany stopped in her tracks, appalled by how easily her mind had slipped into this maze of rationalization. And with a salt-bitter abruptness, she admitted to herself why. She didn't want to believe the worst of Frank Ulring, and there it was. Unable to brush aside the cold boulders of fact, she had rationalized them into mere pebbles. For she couldn't deny, did not even want to deny, his overpowering effect on her. She was a warm and needing woman. And for three years, while the frustrations of her empty marriage had piled up, he had always been there, too vital and dominating and masculine to ignore, gradually infiltrating the vacuum of her needs.

It was even worse, now that Dennis was gone. She was free, and frontier custom which held that long mourning and long widowhood were undesirable still hung on strong in this remote mountain country. She might remarry next week, and few would think the worst of her.

She walked on, her hat dangling by its ribbons from her fingers, and her back was straight. Brace up, Bethany Louisa McAllister. Are you such a lightheaded goose as to leap into the bed of some man because he smiles so handsomely? Brace up! But she felt confused and alone and bitter as she turned up the gravel path to her house.

She unlatched the door and let herself into the *sala*, leaving the door open. A checkering of lamplight from the house across the road penetrated faintly into the room. It lit her way as she crossed to the table, struck a match and lighted the lamp.

'You had better close the door, Miss Bethany.'

A tremor of cool shock ran through her. She half-turned toward the voice, then stood very still.

Will-Joe was sitting on his heels in front of the cold fireplace. His young face was drawn, tired, hollow-cheeked; he would seem gaunted, she supposed, if he weren't ordinarily leaned down to sheer bone and rawhide. His clothes were stained and tattered, and his eyes gleamed with a wild alertness that she saw was not menacing but only a tautly developed habit. His wrists lay on his knees, the hands hanging loose and empty.

'Or,' he said, 'you can yell. I think it would bring a lot of people in a hurry.'

Bethany went to the door and closed it, then drew the blinds on both windows. He stood up and he seemed bigger than she remembered. He smelled of horse and sweat and smoke.

'How did you get in, Will-Joe?'

'The door at the back was not locked. I have only been a few minutes here. I waited for dark.'

'That was wise. But it was foolish of you to come.'

He studied her face. 'You are not afraid?'

'Certainly not.'

'Didn't the sheriff tell you I killed Mr McAllister?'

'Of course, but I believed I knew you well enough to assume it could hardly be deliberate ... murder.' She pointed at his bulky and shapeless right sleeve. 'Is your arm hurt?'

'Yes, ma'am.'

'I will look at it. Sit down. In a chair, please.

155

I'm sure you haven't forgotten how.'

After a moment he moved to the table and pulled out two chairs. He looked at her steadily and a smile brushed her lips. She murmured, 'Or your manners, praise be,' and let him seat her before he stiffly took the chair beside her.

'Lay your arm on the table . . . why did you come here?'

His eyes had not left her face. 'I did not think you would yell,' he said simply.

'No, I am not going to yell, but I'm going to ask some questions.' She had rolled up his sleeve; the soiled and crusted wrapping underneath made her lips tighten. She began to undo it. 'And I expect truthful answers.'

'Yes, teacher.' His soft voice was quite dry.

'Why did you come here, knowing the danger?'

'I wanted you to hear the truth. I don't care what any others think.'

'That's all very well. But the truth . . . that you did not take Dennis's life intentionally? I already believed that.'

'No, that is a lie.' She looked up from his arm and he shook his head. 'I did not kill Mr McAllister. I have killed nobody.'

He talked then. And Bethany listened with an indescribable horror threading her nerve-ends.

She knew she was hearing the truth. Knew it even as a reaction of shocked denial sprang to her lips and died there. Will-Joe was simply

156

telling what had happened. He could not look at her that way and lie. Frank Ulring had killed Dennis. Not by accident, by cold design.

And she knew what even Will-Joe did not. She knew why.

She looked down at the bandage where her fingers now rested motionless. The strip of calico was dried to the flesh of his arm, but there was no bloodstain.

'I will have to soak this off,' she said.

Mechanically she went to the kitchen and lighted a lamp and touched a match to the pyre of kindling in the iron range. She set a pan of water on to boil and stood looking at it, thinking that she was in a nightmare that was real.

Real, and all too clear. Frank had broken his promise to her because he couldn't afford to do otherwise. Will-Joe was a deadly witness. One whose story could ruin Frank even if his word were disbelieved in a court of law. She did not even have to ask herself whether Frank were capable of setting up an elaborate plan to murder her husband. She knew Frank, knew beyond any doubt that he could do exactly what he deemed necessary to get whatever he wanted. She looked at the flimsy straws of her former rationalizations of his character: they broke and crumbled, they were nothing.

She carried a basin of hot water back to the table and dipped a cloth and began to soak away Will-Joe's caked bandage. It loosened at once and she peeled it off, taking the poultice

157

with it. She was surprised to see that the deep grooved wound was hardly inflamed or swollen at all, and that healing had begun.

'Did you make this poultice?'

'No. Rainbow Girl, two days ago.'

'What's in it, do you know?'

He shrugged. 'Prickly pear ... different herbs. She is a medicine woman, she knows the secrets. I don't think she would tell you.'

'That's a pity. Well ...' She ran the hot cloth over his arm again and examined the clean line of healing. 'I think now it will heal faster with no bandage. Will-Joe—'

'Ma'am?'

'Do you know why the sheriff did what he did?'

He looked at her a long moment, caught by her intensity, and she saw his understanding. 'I think maybe so.'

'Say it then.'

'It is because of you.'

'Yes.'

She rose and patted his shoulder as she passed behind his chair and went to the front window. She pulled back the edge of the blind and looked down the road at the town lights.

'Do you have a horse?'

'Outside of town.'

'Then you had better get to him. And ride as far away as you can.' She turned and met his eyes. 'Don't come back, Will-Joe. I ask you as a friend.'

158

He pushed back the chair and stood. He clasped his wrist and stared at the wound, and then he looked up. 'I didn't think before about why he did it. You are not safe.'

She forced a smile. 'He can't do anything to me . . . you're the one in danger.'

'You, too.' A quiet stubborness pinched his cheeks. 'If it would help, I can stand trial. It would all come out then, what he did.'

'But there's no proof. Except your word—' She hesitated.

'The white man's law is for white men.'

'Yes, and you would be obliged to give yourself up to the sheriff. You'd wait trial in his jail. You see?'

'There would never be a trial.' He shook his head. 'But the mountains are my home. He will not find me in them. Unless I let him.'

Alarm flared in her. She could only look at him wordlessly, helplessly.

'I will not run from him again, Miss Bethany.'

CHAPTER TWELVE

Will-Joe left the McAllister house as he had entered it, by the back door. He stepped out into the quiet darkness and heard Miss Bethany's soft admonition to be careful. And she closed the door behind him. He stood

159

listening a moment, picking out no particular sound and yet aware of a hundred distinct sounds, voices of the night.

He cut to his right through the darkness, going across an adjacent yard almost at a crouch through the brush and weed tangles. He had left his horse back in some trees at the other end of town. Close to the road, on the chance he might have to get away fast. At the same time, against any possibility of the animal being discovered, he hadn't wanted to leave him near Miss Bethany's home. If he should be seen getting away, it was important for her sake that nobody guess he had come to visit her.

He was glad he had come and that she had listened well. It had made any risk worth the while. It was all-important that she, of all people, believed in him. More: she was warned against a danger that he had not previously considered. How could he have been so stupid as not to realize Ulring's motive for murder? True, she would know worry now—but better to be aware of a danger and perhaps be able to fight it.

Perhaps she was right and she personally had nothing to fear from Ulring. But Will-Joe wasn't so sure. *Tsi Tsosi* was a man to go after what he wanted with a one-track fury. And if he couldn't get it one way . . .

Close by, a dog began to bark.

Will-Joe came to a dead stop and slipped down on his haunches in the weeds. He couldn't see the dog; had it picked him up? The barking ceased now, but as he moved on it resumed again, even more furiously. Will-Joe lifted into a half-trot, crossing another yard slantwise. He wanted to skirt wide of the main street, at the same time keeping toward the rear of the buildings wherever he could.

The dog was coming after him, the barking getting closer. Then it was racing at his heels, a light-colored feist of a mutt who worried his legs furiously. Its feral, shrill yapping was enough to raise half the town.

A couple houses to Will-Joe's back, a door opened; light streamed out. 'Mustard!' a man called.

Will-Joe hauled up under a shadowy clump of cottonwood and turned, pulling his knife. Would he have to kill the dog to shut it up? Mustard began veering back and forth and around him, snapping at his shins.

He swung at the animal. It leaped away and stood a few yards off, barking and bristling. Another door banged open; a man sleepily demanded what the hell was going on.

Will-Joe shrank away from the trees and swung toward the main street, away from the residential area. He had to move at a gingerly pace in the dark, and Mustard followed him. Its owner called again, adding some choice expletives. Mustard broke off and trotted away, satisfied that it had put the run on a prowler.

Will-Joe pushed on as fast as he dared, his

senses pitched to a hard tingling alertness. No telling how many people, curious about the racket, would be coming to their doors. The moon had emerged from behind a cloud bank; it burst across the landscape like a silvery lamp. In the open now, Will-Joe could distinguish details clearly; he picked up speed, but kept in the shadow behind a row of main street buildings. He was running as he came past a corner.

He slammed full-tilt into a man coming through the alley. Their bodies collided head-on and smashed together, knocking both of them sprawling.

Will-Joe lay stunned on his belly for several moments, sparks pinwheeling in his eyes. Then, getting his hands under him, he pushed to his feet, grabbing at the wall for support. He looked down at the man groaning on the ground. Liquid was gurgling from a bottle; he had a raw ripe whiff of it. A drunk, he thought. The man had come staggering up the alley to finish his bottle in the weeds at the back.

Still dazed, Will-Joe pushed away from the wall, stepped over the drunk and moved on. He tried to hurry, but he had banged his knee somehow; all he could manage was an awkward shuffle.

The livery corral was just ahead, and he made a swing outward to avoid it, but the smell or sound of him disturbed the horses. They began snorting and milling. A lantern bobbed in the rear archway of the barn, throwing out a saffron pool of light.

'Who's that there? What're you doing?'

It was Claude Warhoon's voice, and now Claude spotted him in the open moonlight and yelled: 'Hold up there!' He pounded out of the archway at a run, skirting around the corral. Will-Joe saw light streak the barrel of a pistol in his fist.

He limped furiously on, but the thud of feet told him Claude was coming too fast, and now he pulled his own pistol and wheeled. Claude pulled up about ten yards away. He held the lantern high.

'Who'n hell are . . . Jesus! It's—'

His arm straightened; Will-Joe heard the metallic rasp as a pistol hammer was eared back. He melted to the ground as the gun roared. Claude fired again. The shot was low and wide, but it flung dirt over him.

He did not think. It was no time to think. His arm was cramped against his side with his pistol and he arced it around and up, and saw Claude's shape blot darkly beyond the sights, and he shot.

Claude grunted and dropped the lantern. Then he was going boneless and falling, and his body toppled across the lantern.

Will-Joe scrambled up. He limped on toward the trees that hid his horse, the sweat cold as ice on his body. He heard another voice yelling now. And that was Ulring's.

Ulring was slumped deep in his saddle, almost half-dozing as he rode into town from the north. Christ, but he was tired. His mind clutched at ragtag ends of thought that kept slipping from his mental grasp. Anger and frustration beset him. And gut-deep exhaustion. Some learned bastard ought to write a treatise on the anatomy of exhaustion, he thought. The kind of dead aching fatigue that ate into every pore of a man's being. A thing as much of the mind as of the body. For a man driven toward an insensate goal could never rest; his obsession wore at him as steadily as did his physical fury.

He had not wanted to return to town, but he had reached his limit. His senses kept whirling into a sick dead blur; his body was almost numb to sensation. He was too used up to register normal impressions any longer—much less maintain the trigger-pitch of alertness he needed. The goddam proverbial needle in the hay had nothing on that siwash kid. And if he did get lucky and suddenly encounter him, the kid would have all the edge. Hell! He needed a hot bath, a filling meal, and about twenty hours in a good bed. Then—

The shots whacked like the cracks of a bullwhip across the night. Two of them, spaced a little apart.

Ulring straightened, looking around. He shook the fog from his brain. He was almost abreast of the livery barn, and his mind raced back and evaluated the sounds. Gunshots? Close ... damned close ... just beyond the barn.

He dropped to the ground and ran for the livery archway, pulling his gun. He stopped inside the barn. A big lantern slung from a peg threw out a rancid glow. Nobody here. He moved down the runway. Horses stamped restively; the hot close stinks of the barn, dung and straw and ammonia, surrounded him. He passed through the far archway and halted again.

'Anyone out there?'

Abruptly then, he heard a horse running. He broke into a run, cutting around the corral. He saw a man's body darkly crumpled against the dusty moon sheen of the ground. And froze, gun out and up, listening. But the tattoo of hoofs was already dying away in the night.

Ulring went on a few steps, then halted and knelt, turning the body over. Metal tinkled; a coal oil stench rose. Moonlight hit the dead face. Claude. His torn throat glistened with a black wetness. A bullet must have gone through his jugular.

Ulring sized it at once. Claude had heard something suspicious and had come out with the lantern. Ulring took the gun from his limp hand and sniffed it. The first shot had been Claude's, and he had missed. The prowler, whoever it was, hadn't.

Who had it been? *Maybe*, Ulring thought. A

small rising excitement bristled the hairs on the back of his neck. Maybe. Claude wasn't the type to cut down on a mere prowler. And even if it hadn't been the kid . . . who was to say?

Voices from the street. Men were gathering out there, asking questions. A smile tightened his mouth. He would give them a few answers. He straightened up and holstered his gun, gazing down at the body a speculative moment. Then he rammed Claude's gun into his belt under the skirt of his coat and tramped back into the barn and out to the street. He headed for the knot of men pulling together in the outspilling light in front of the Pink Lady.

'Here comes . . . hey, it's Ulring,' someone said.

'Frank!' Bert Stang hailed him. 'You hear them shots?'

Ulring reached the group. He ran a grim eye over their faces, then jerked his head backward toward the barn. 'Claude's back there. One of you come with me. We'll fetch him in.'

'Jeez,' a man twanged. 'Claude get hurt?'

'He's dead,' Ulring said quietly. 'It was that breed bastard. He shot Claude dead. I saw it.'

*   *   *

'I don't believe it,' Bethany said.

Ulring ran a thumb along his mustache, then dropped his hand heavily to his knee. He gazed at her face, trying to discern what lay behind it.

166

She was pale but composed. The slim hands knotted together in her lap were white-knuckled with strain. He leaned forward a little, the leather-rigged chair creaking to his weight.

'Beth, what do you want to hear? What else can I tell you? I rode in, I heard the shot. I saw the kid bending over Claude's body—'

'You saw him?'

'Square under the moon, plain as day. He cut and ran. I shot at him and missed and he got to his horse. Lord, Claude wasn't even armed.'

'You told me.'

She rose and walked across the parlor and back, kneading her hands together, not looking at him. Ulring got to his feet and stared at her, his eyes cold and baffled.

'No mistake this time. It was plain damned cold-blooded murder. I guess that doesn't matter to you.'

'Frank, stop it!' She whirled to face him, her throat muscles flexing. 'Of course it matters. I liked Claude. What do you expect of me?'

'That you quit making excuses for that murdering breed.'

She bit her lip and frowned at her hands. 'I think, Frank, that you had better leave.'

'Beth, Lord A'mighty.' He spread his big hands palms up. 'I didn't mean to be rude, but look—I don't mean to sound brutal either— you have to stop finding excuses for that kid.

Listen, it's understandable. I'm a stubborn lad myself. When I've been wrong about someone, I have a hard time bringing myself to admit it.'

'Do you?' Her gaze lifted and locked his: her eyes were like clear crystal. 'Not a very pleasant feeling, is it?'

Something in it struck him curiously. His right fist at his side crushed gently around the brim of his hat. 'You know, I wonder something. What Cantrell was doing in town. I hadn't really thought about it.'

'I suppose he had his reasons.'

'You never know about an Injun.' He watched her face. 'But he's not dumb, is he? You said so. Now sneaking back to a place full of his enemies. That's dumb. Course he could have been looking to steal food. If he was white, I'd even count it likely. But a siwash like that, he could live off the country easy as not.'

'Frank, do you mind? I'm rather tired . . .'

'Did he come here to see you?' He shot the words like bullets. 'Is that it, Beth?'

'Don't be ridiculous.'

His stare whiplashed her face: it was smooth as pale china. Her tone was tart and faintly impatient, and he could read nothing else into it. If he was here, Ulring thought, he gave you an earful. You'd only lie about it if you believed him.

Aloud, he said calmly: 'Well, it was just a thought. He was heap big protégé of yours, and I had the idea he thought as much of you as you

168

did of him.'

'You'd have to ask him about that, Frank.'

'Have to find him first.' He grinned crookedly and walked to the door, clapping his hat on his head. 'G'night, Beth . . .'

He headed slowly toward his office. She knew. No mar to her dissembling, but he was sure of it. If for no better reason than that her reaction had been too finely controlled, altogether too natural to be believable. Prepared. She must be afraid, too, and had hidden it perfectly. Afraid . . . she had a right to be. Ulring slowed; his fingers curled into his palms. Fury like a white-hot light flooded his mind. He wanted to turn back, to take her white throat between his hands and shake it out of her. He wanted to . . .

No. Let it go. He was in deep enough already. First came the kid. He had been in town tonight, Ulring felt unshakably sure—he had seen Bethany, he had shot Claude. Earlier, he had been worrying that the kid had fled the country. He did not want that; it was a loose end. He wanted everything tied up securely. Already the kid had talked. To Bloodgood. Now to Bethany.

It was like a noose drawing perceptibly tighter, and time was running out. Now his cherished goal was slipping away: Bethany. No, by God! She was his. Would be, one way or the other. If, in the end, he couldn't have her, no other man would.

First he had to get that goddam kid. But could he? Another posse was his for the asking, and this time they would stick: everyone had liked Claude, and the second killing had crystalized a certainty that nobody was safe with a breed killer at large. Everyone was all wrought up. But the quarry had proved too elusive and too lucky up till now, and he might well continue to be.

Ulring tramped onto the porch of his office, unlocked the door and lighted the wall lamp. He closed the door and went to his desk and dropped into the swivel chair. His arms felt like dead weights as he took Claude's gun from his belt, opened a drawer and laid it inside, afterward lifting out a bottle of whiskey and a glass. He poured a drink and stared heavily at the wall. Christ . . . tired. His thoughts were like congealed glue. Better sleep on all of it. He slapped the cork back in the bottle and started to return it to the drawer.

The latch clicked. His nerves jumped like released springs. His eyes flew to the door. It was moving slowly ajar. His hand moved into the open drawer and closed over Claude's pistol. When the door had opened a foot, Caspar Bloodgood came sideways through it.

'How-do, boy.'

'What the hell are you doing here?'

'You got a memory needs weeding out.' Bloodgood padded halfway across the room and dropped on his haunches facing the desk,

170

rifle across his knees. 'Catched myself some firewater at Stang's pizen parlor. Catched an earful too. Heerd you folks hit a chuckhole of excitement.'

'Listen, old man—'

'I'm talking. Come down day before yestiday, but you wa'n't about. Heerd you found the kid where I figgered, hey?'

'All right, then you heard he got away.'

'No fault o' mine you couldn't pluck a goose you got handed on a platter. Wa'n't nothing said 'bout whether you got him. Pony up.'

Ulring's fingers twitched with a raw impulse. He damped it down and slid the drawer gently shut, then rubbed a fist along his jaw. He stared thoughtfully at the mountain man.

'All right. It slipped my mind, and that's the truth. But you'll have to wait till morning. When the bank opens, I'll get your five hundred dollars.'

Bloodgood chuckled rustily. 'Billy-be-damn right you will. Only I'd hazard there's a whoop'n' a holler more'n that sitting in your craw.'

'You think so?'

'I told you that Injun son 'ud have you jaspers eating your own dust. I 'low it has got through to you that you ain't gonna tree no red coon 'thout proper help. You are singing softer.'

Ulring smiled. 'Like a book, Caspar. That's how you read me. All right, let's not spar

171

words. Five hundred in the morning, as agreed. Another five hundred when you've brought me his scalp.'

Bloodgood shook his head. His hat canted deeply over his brow, putting one eye in shadow; the other gleamed like a knife. 'Take more'n, that, sonny. I been talking around, putting bits'n' pieces together. I 'low I have cinched onto why you wanted McAllister dead. It's that woman o' his, ain't it? That's a reason a heap o' folks might believe if it was to get told about you done for that dude your own self.'

'I see.' Ulring grooved his underlip with a thumb. 'Keep-still money, is it? A thousand after the job—for the kid *and* your silence. That's flat; not a dollar more. I'll have to float a loan as it is. Take it or leave it.'

'Sure, sonny. I ain't greedy. Fifteen hunnerd'll bind my jaw tighter'n a swig of alkali juice.'

'It won't be easy. He'll have guessed it was you that tipped me off about him being in John Thunder's village.'

Bloodgood's beard split in a stained grin. 'Shoot, sonny, you leave me worry 'bout that. I 'uz coming t' town 'long the north road when I heard them two shots. Pulled offen the road when I heard some 'un coming like they was a burr up his ass. Kid lit out past me so close I could 'most a touched him.'

'You saw him—you had a chance—'

'This child never pizened a varmint that

172

don't clear bounty. How you want his scalp cured, cousin?'

'You can leave it on him,' Ulring said coldy. 'When you come for the rest of your money, you'll take me to where the body is. When I've seen it, I'll hand you the balance. The thing is, Bloodgood, I want the kid to just drop out of sight. Let people guess. I don't want him found . . . ever.'

'Purely shines.' Bloodgood got up and walked to the door. 'Don't you fret, boy. That breed's hide is as good as nailed up. See you in the morning.'

He went out, softly closing the door behind him.

CHAPTER THIRTEEN

Will-Joe usually woke the way an animal did, all his senses bristling to focus at once. This morning he opened his eyes and ran his gaze up and around through the trees, touching everything in its range before he moved a muscle.

He had made his camp in the bottom of a steep canyon. It did not box off, for he had gotten in the habit of choosing his bivouacs with an eye to more than mere seclusion. The canyon ran for a half mile before its walls tapered down, but a man could slip out at either end. The west wall soared almost vertically for a couple hundred feet: a sheer lift of crumbling discolored sandstone painted to fiery hues by morning sunrays that had not yet penetrated to the canyon depths. The other wall was more of a deep slant, overgrown by scrub cedar that had taken tenacious root among the strewings of giant boulders.

Will-Joe threw off his single blanket and rose in one movement, stretching. He had gotten a good night's sleep burrowed in a heap of dry soft sand. He shook the grains out of his hair and clothes, and glanced at the pinto that Rainbow Girl had given him. He had tethered the animal on a skimpy patch of galleta grass and now, roused from sleep, it began to eat.

There was little forage available for Will-Joe himself, a fact that did not cause him immediate concern. He had spent yesterday fashioning a rawhide-string bow and some arrows, hardening the tips in a small fire. He was tired of living off wild truck. Maybe today he could bag a rabbit. The brush downcanyon was threaded with runways. He would set some snares too. He was still leery of firing off his pistol and he wanted to conserve shells, but he had now spent two days in the canyon and he felt an undeniable security.

The canyon bottom was laced with heavy cover; cottonwoods and willows flourished in the damp sand along most of its length. His camp was well hidden from any direction,

174

including from above, and he had taken considerable pains to hide his trail coming here. The canyon was remote from any sort of human habitation, for it had to be approached over the roughest kind of country. He had remembered it from years ago, when he and Adakhai had camped here on a hunting trip.

It was nice here. A man could think; he could weigh his moves, sift his plans and wonder what to do next.

He still hadn't arrived at anything definite. His determination to hang on somehow, to try to prove his innocence, had waned. He still hated the idea of running, but after two nights ago and the stroke of bad luck that had brought Claude Warhoon blundering out to his death, the whole picture had been clouded. His bullet had killed Claude; he was sure of it.

Claude had never been his enemy. Occasionally, when he'd lived in town and eked out a living while attending Miss Bethany's school, he and Claude had chummed together. Claude was happy-go-lucky, unshackled by color pride or by much of anything except his lazy devotion to Sheriff Ulring, whom he regarded as a great man. Intelligence was not one of Claude's strong points either, but there had been no malice in him, not a shred of resentment even at those times when Will-Joe had beaten him in getting one or other of the odd jobs on which both had depended.

Claude. The killing hollowed Will-Joe's belly

with a sick regret. He had not wanted to shoot at Claude who—knowing how furiously his idol Ulring had pursued this particular fugitive—had simply acted in blind innocence. But there'd been no choice, no time for anything but to cut down fast on Claude's blurred form.

Nobody had seen it, of course. Nobody could be sure who had done it . . . unless Claude had lived long enough to give his name. That was a possibility. But even if not, he would be a natural suspect. Lacking a shred of real evidence, the good people of Spurlock would be happy, as they hasseled over the pros and cons of how it might have happened, to stretch their imaginations enough to accommodate a breed fugitive. Miss Bethany would easily guess at how and why Claude had been killed, and she would understand. And, he was sure, she would say nothing.

All this was guessing, but he was pretty sure it would go something like that. As for the little matter of his having shot in self-defense, the law would not care: it made no allowance for any fugitive from its implacable code.

Perhaps it really made little difference, so long as he could not prove himself guiltless of McAllister's death. He had hung on here partly out of a desire to convince Miss Bethany of his innocence. That much he had accomplished—but it was small satisfaction now that he knew of Ulring's real design. The wolf and the rabbit. She was forewarned—what more could he do?

Unless.

Unless he turned the hunt back on Ulring, matching his brain and skills against the sheriff's. One bullet would end the threat to Miss Bethany. And he'd be no worse off than he had been; they could only hang him once. They had to catch him first, and once he had a good start out of the country . . .

The infuriating hitch was, he wanted to stay. For reasons that had grown increasingly confusing even to his own mind. But reasons he couldn't ignore.

Picking up a stone, he pegged it furiously into the dead fire. 'Damn!' His frustration and impatience shaped a white man's epithet . . . but it was Indian fatalism that made him shrug his shoulders then. He needed to do some more thinking, that was all.

At a point a hundred feet below his camp, the groundwater pooled on the surface and formed a little spring. He might as well fill his belly with water and call it breakfast; he wasn't particularly hungry anyway. A man's gut shrank below need when it subsisted on the sort of inadequate fare he had been supplying it. He needed meat, chunky pieces of spit-broiled meat, and plenty of it. He could afford the time and care necessary to stalk it.

He walked a short distance downcanyon through the trees, halting when the cover began to thin away. The spring was cupped in a rocky trough another two hundred feet out. He would have to cross the open to reach it, and he made a habit of checking his surroundings before leaving the trees. The morning was serene. Weak sunlight touched his face; a hawk pivoted on the pale bowl of sky. Nothing else moved. Birds were twittering the morning to life, rustling unseen through the low growth of weeds and bushes on the canyon bottom and higher up on the sloping east wall.

Will-Joe crossed to the spring, knelt beside it, cupped his hands and drank. The water had a brittle iron flavor that was not exactly displeasing. It was so cold it made his teeth ache. He ducked his head and raised it, throwing back his wet hair. Then grew tight-muscled, though for an instant only.

Some birds on the slope had ceased their rustling and chirpings. A minor-key but specific break in the gentle blend of diurnal sounds. Something or someone up there, maybe someone in hiding, had moved enough to alarm the birds. It might mean nothing; it could mean anything.

Again he was the hunted: nerve-poised, ready.

His pause of realization was imperceptible. He continued the easy normalcy of his movements, even ducked his head again, letting the water sluice down inside his shirt. Rising then, he tramped back toward the trees. He made himself walk slowly. Once in the trees, he could not be seen. And his pistol was there, stowed in his gear.

He was fifty feet from the trees when a voice called. 'Freeze right there, boy. I got a bead square on your head.'

He came to a dead stop, not even turning his head. No need to. He knew Bloodgood's voice and knew too that he was so close, he could plunk a squirrel's eye at this distance without half-trying.

Bloodgood rose, a lean shadow among the rocks halfway up the slope, and came down easy as a goat. He tramped up to Will-Joe, looking a little red-eyed. His rifle was cradled under one bent arm, held in a casual aim, hand ready to the trigger.

'Boy, you are a smart 'un. You don't gotta die just yet.'

He reached out and lifted Will-Joe's knife from its sheath, then motioned with a lazy sweep of the rifle barrel. Will-Joe walked ahead of him to the camp in the trees. Bloodgood made him stretch out on the ground face down and then, muttering to himself, poked through Will-Joe's few belongings.

'If you ain't a piddling pack rat. Little o' this, little o' that. Boy, ain't you a hair curious how I found you?'

'I am surprised you had a reason to.'

'Thousand dollar hain't a bad reason.' Bloodgood's chuckle grated like a rusty saw. 'Hell, ain't nothing here worth a man's time picking up. 'Cep'n this.' He hefted Will-Joe's pistol, and glanced at the pinto. 'Maybe him too. Good-looking hoss. That the one your little klootch give you? Heerd about that. Roll over and stick your hands up front of you.'

Bloodgood had a rope coiled over his arm. He shook it out, then moved over to Will-Joe, slipped the noose over his wrists and yanked it tight, took a few quick turns and tightened them, then made a knot. Afterward he cut off a couple lengths of the other end, put a hackamore on the pinto, unhobbled him, fastened on a lead-rope and then boosted Will-Joe to the animal's back.

Leading the pinto, Bloodgood walked the quarter mile to the north outlet of the canyon. He had a big rawboned jughead of a paint horse tethered in some brush there. He tied the lead-rope to the horn of the paint's scarred and shiny-worn saddle, then swung astride.

'Well, boy, we got a passel of rough riding to do. Best clamp that pinto's barrel with your knees and hang tight.'

Will-Joe was puzzled. 'Mr Bloodgood . . . did the sheriff pay you to find me?'

'Sonny, didn't you cinch onto that right off?'

'It does not make sense that he would want me brought in for trial . . . where I can tell my story.'

'Why, bless you, boy, course he don't. Not on your tintype.'

'Then why take the trouble to take me

anywhere else?' Will-Joe said it with an atonal flatness. 'I can die as easy right here.'

'Shuckins, ain't no argufying that,' Bloodgood said genially. He kicked his horse into motion, talking across his shoulder as they rode: 'But I got to show him your carcass afore I get paid. Sight easier to herd you back near town afore I dust you off. Otherwise I got to fetch the sheriff clear back here and that is a tol'able piece of distance.'

'Yes. But you tracked me so far.'

'Yep, for all you did to hide your sign like an ole scout. You just fetched up agin the wrong bearcat, sonny. I 'uz tracking red coon for the Army when your pappy was a pup. Hell, I was squatting right off the road when you cut out t'other night after dusting that Claude feller. Was you done that, wa'n't it? Could of tetched you, I was that close.'

'But the sheriff had to make it worth your while.'

'Don't take a pile of figgering, do it? So I cut your track from there. Give me a blamed hard time, I got to own. You kiver trail smart. Stuck on ground rougher'n a razorback's bristles. Doubled back and looped around more'n an ole fox running hounds. Blame near threw me. Took me two day at that. Come on that canyon sunset yestiday. Seen a thread o' smoke. Just a thread, but you shoulda knowed better'n to build any kind o' fire.'

'No. That was a mistake.'

181

'I spotted things pret' well, but being I couldn't make you out in them trees, I didn't aim to sneak in and maybe have you throw down on me. So I hunkered up on the slope above the spring and waited for you come get a drink. Lot o' trouble, but I figgered I best see you afore you seen me.' Bloodgood scraped another chuckle. 'Knowed you wouldn't be leaving out no latchstring for ole Caspar.'

'Not after Sheriff Ulring came with others to the Navajo camp,' Will-Joe said thinly. 'He did that like he knew. Like someone told him.'

'Some 'un did, sonny . . .'

They crossed a short stony valley and began climbing a hogback ridge, following roughly the route by which Will-Joe had come to the canyon. It was parched and broken country. Scrub timber clung in desolate patches to the slopes and crowns of almost barren ridges. There was little flat terrain; the valleys between ridges veed into cramped pockets that formed a cross-hatching of brief canyons and washes. It made for slow, hard going even if a man were not systematically covering his own trail or uncovering another's.

Will-Joe guessed that with no delays, it would take at least a full day to reach Spurlock. And Bloodgood did not intend to take him quite that far . . . which meant that he still had perhaps nine or ten hours of life. Long cruel hours. It was hard to keep a seat on the bareback pinto, straining for balance and nothing but his dug-in heels and his hands gripping the mane to hold him upright. Already his hands were going numb from the bite of ropes that Bloodgood had yanked savagely tight. Long before they got to wherever the mountain man was taking him, he would be senseless with pain and fatigue.

They climbed steadily through the ridges. The country would get progressively rougher until the ridges dwindled away into the deep smooth valleys of the foothill country above Spurlock. The old game and Indian trails which most white men would not even recognize twisted in grotesque hairpins around spired rocks and along canyon rims; they switchbacked up and down a corduroy of rugged ridges.

Will-Joe flexed his hands and rolled his wrists against the ropes; the fibers drew blood and rasped the flesh raw, but he worked some feeling back into his fingers. A nerve of desperation threaded his belly like hot wire. Soon, very soon, if there was any chance at all . . .

They began the descent of a long height that dropped almost sheer into a narrow gorge. The trail down clung like an irregular ribbon to the wall, but it was a fairly wide trail, formed by a natural fault which Indians of a bygone age had widened by patient chipping with flint tools. Still it was treacherous going, for the shale was rotted by ancient weathering, scaling away in sizable chunks. The wall above was scarred and pitted, the trail littered with pieces of fallaway rock, and the lip of the ledge that formed the trail was either crumbling away or hanging in brittle stubs that it would take very little to dislodge. The gorge below was strewn with chunks fallen from above.

Giving the pinto a slow pressure of the knee, Will-Joe edged him closer to the brink. He peered over. Mountain-bred, he had no fear of height; he judged that the wall dropped fifty feet to the gorge floor. The pinto side-shuffled nervously, his hoofs skittering fragments of rock. They rolled off the brink and clattered downward.

Bloodgood, picking his way carefully just ahead, turned in his saddle. 'Gawdammit, boy, keep that nag up next the wall.'

Will-Joe lightly drummed the pinto's flank with his right heel, nudging him back to the inner trail. The wall was laced with shallow crevices and sharp-angled shelves. His eye fastened on a loose shard of rock on a shelf eye-level to him a few yards ahead. As he pulled abreast of it, he thudded the pinto's barrel on the right side, making him press so close to the wall that Will-Joe's left knee rasped painfully against it. He swept his bound hands up and sideways, closed them around the rock fragment and brought it down.

He kept his eyes on Bloodgood's back, waiting, hugging the hunk of jagged shale between his crotch and the horse's neck. His heart slugged fiercely at his ribs as he waited for the mountain man to acknowledge that he had detected something amiss. But Bloodgood didn't look back.

He rode slowly on. The trail plunged at a deep slant now; the horses picked their way haltingly across the rubble. Will-Joe flexed and unflexed his sweating hands around the rock. About six inches long, it fit his grip like a tool, smooth as glass and just as sharp where the rough corners gouged his palm, and it tapered down to a chisel edge.

Just ahead, Will-Joe knew, the ledge narrowed somewhat and made a sharp twist; then it was clear going to the bottom. His muscles corded with tension.

Now?

The littered steepness of the trail was making Bloodgood's jughead skittish. He flattened his ears and fiddlefooted, quartering partly around. The old man swore, leaned across the animal's neck and chopped a bony fist against his muzzle.

'Settle down, you wall-eyed bastard, or I'll bust your nose like a ripe tomater—'

Now.

Will-Joe drove both heels into the pinto's sides. He gigged forward with a stiff-legged fright, almost barreling into Bloodgood's mount before he swung aside, then pulled up hard. The horses were a couple feet apart, flank to flank.

Bloodgood fought to control his quaking animal. His red-eyed glance whipped Will-Joe's face. 'Don't crowd me, gawdam you, boy!'

His eyes dropped. He saw the heavy sliver of stone clenched between Will-Joe's hands. His mouth opened. His hands were occupied with the reins and he could not even begin to grab at the Winchester jutting up under his knee as Will-Joe's bound hands lifted.

Instead he grabbed at Will-Joe's arm as if to deflect an intended blow at his head. It was a mistake. For Will-Joe arced the rock down with all his strength at the opposite shoulder of his own horse.

The chisel edge cut low and deep into the muscle swell just below the pinto's wither. The animal leaped sidelong as if hit by hot iron, away from the source of pain. He slammed full force into the jughead, shoulder point catching him above the girth: a pivotal smash of weight against weight that drove the jughead helplessly sideways.

The jughead's legs crumpled, he was going down, and as he fell, his flailing hoofs hit the slick rimrock. Will-Joe saw the shocked blur of Bloodgood's face an instant before they went over, horse and rider together, and heard a hoarse dwindling shriek as they vanished.

He had time for that one clear impression. Then he was clinging like a burr to the pinto's back as he spun and reared in panic. His back hoofs skidded on the rim. Rock crumbled. He scrambled wildly as he began to slip, forehoofs striking for solid footing, shuddering with convulsive effort. His hind-quarters went over the brink, then his whole body.

Will-Joe pushed out with his legs away from the falling animal. But he was falling too.

He plunged helplessly down the slanting drop, his body battered like a bouncing cork, till he hit a rounded knob of rock that shelved out from the wall. Hit it with his doubled left leg. Heard the bone crack like dry wood. Screamed with the scarlet pain that mushroomed through his body.

For a moment he hung across the rounded shelf, his legs hanging over. Falling rubble showered his body. Then he was slipping off, his consciousness ebbing away on an excruciating rush of pain and shock. And a tide of final blackness as he fell . . .

CHAPTER FOURTEEN

Sensation returned in a hot slow trickling. He was face down, he was sure of that ahead of anything. His skull throbbed terribly and his throat felt like a raw kiln. Then awareness poured back in a blinding flood and he groaned.

Will-Joe had fallen partly across the body of

his horse. It had broken his fall somewhat. That, and the fact that he had not landed on any of the flinty strewings that pocked the gorge bottom. His forehead rested on hot soft earth and he raised his head and groaned again. He flattened his bound hands against the ground and pushed his torso up. A cloud of flies rose, buzzing angrily. There was more pain, but his mind steeled against it. Moving his left leg caused a wrench of agony that made him grow still again.

A fuddled ribbon of memory told him that he had hit that leg in falling. He moved the other leg carefully. It was all right, he was battered raw from head to foot, but he could move everything except that leg. Broken? He would have to see.

He put all his strength into the effort of turning his body over. He set his teeth and heaved, and rolled sideways off the carcass of his horse. The slight jar as he lit on his back shot an eruption of agony from his leg through his body and beat in red ripples against his brain. His eyes blurred. He fought the waves of rising darkness and held his teeth clenched till the worst of it subsided. Then he raised himself on his elbows and looked.

Broken. Yes. He could see the slight angle made by shattered bone through his pantsleg. The break was halfway between knee and ankle, but he could not tell anything more.

He turned his head till he could see the

188

bodies of Caspar Bloodgood and his horse. They were to the rear of him, only a few yards away. A great brown stain matted Bloodgood's gray hair and dyed the rock under his head. His legs were pinned by his horse and an occasional convulsive shudder ran through the animal; it was alive.

Will-Joe lifted his face. They had been on a deep slant of the trail, but still over forty feet above the gorge floor. It wasn't quite a straight drop, as his lacerated body testified. His clothes were shredded, clotted with dried blood, and his body felt like one vast bruise. The knob he had hit with his leg, he realized, may have saved his life. Projecting about fifteen feet below the rim, it had stopped his fall completely at that point. The sharp fragments littering the bottom had proved as fatal to his horse and Bloodgood as the slanting fall itself.

He blinked at the sky. How long had he been here? It was still full daylight, but he could not see the sun. It had been early morning when they had gone over the rim and the sun had not been high; shadow had still filled the gorge. It must be late in the day now, the sun having arced completely overhead and out of sight, for the sand was warm, yet the gorge was shadow-filled again.

His attention came back to his leg. He felt a rush of fear for it that, for the moment, eclipsed every other concern. Again he steeled himself and braved the anguish of tortured flesh to flop over on his belly. Digging in his elbows, he pulled himself along by straining, jerking inches till he reached Bloodgood's corpse. He pulled the mountain man's big bone-handled knife from its sheath and reversed it between his hands so the blade's razor edge rested on the ropes. Using only his fingers, he sawed it back and forth till the strands parted. Turning on his back once more, he eased himself up by agonized degrees to a sitting position. With the knife he tore the seam of his pantsleg apart from the knee down.

The lower leg was like a rubbery sausage, swollen to almost twice its normal width. It was discolored a purplish-black hue and the flesh was a mangle of red jelly where it had hit the rock. He kneaded it around the break, fighting the pain that made him want to jerk his fingers back. There it was . . . a sharp ridge of broken bone, but not a clean break.

He thought of only one thing then. Not of escape from this deep trap of a chasm, not of his burning thirst or even of the sweetness of life itself. But only that if his leg healed thus, he would be a cripple for the rest of his days.

He had to set it. But how? He felt weak and sick, his stomach churning. He doubted he could summon the strength to do it with his hands. Even if he could, he would probably pass out before the job was done.

Will-Joe looked around. His eyes settled on

two large rocks that lay almost together, a space of two inches between them at their closest point. That might do it. But he had to get everything ready.

He looked around again. The nearest clump of brush was at the base of the wall some twenty feet away. That would have to do. With Bloodgood's knife he hacked away a piece of Bloodgood's hunting coat and sliced the buckskin into thin strips. He stuffed these inside his shirt and shoved the knife into his sheath and looked at the brush clump again.

Grinding his jaws, Will-Joe set his elbows in and began to inch his way toward it. Cutting the tough leather had been a struggle; it had taken a good deal out of him. The pain was slugging like a rising-falling knife at the base of his skull, and suddenly the contents of his belly rushed into his throat. He stopped and retched. Retched again. And moved on, his body soaked with sweat.

He rested a minute after reaching the brush. He hacked off two tall wands as thick as his thumb and cut each one into three equal-length pieces. He tucked these into his belt and then began a grueling crawl toward the rocks. It took him five minutes to reach them.

He maneuvered himself into position on his back and carefully lowered the ankle of his broken leg between the rocks, turning his foot so the instep and heel were firmly wedged. He lay flat and reached back and caught hold of another sizable rock and arched his body almost clear of the ground. He pulled suddenly.

Pain blazed. This time it was too much, and he passed out completely.

He was unconscious for a minute or less. When he came to, he lay quietly, sweating, flexing his fingers. He had to straighten that leg, no matter what it took.

He rested another minute, pulling his mind and body together for a supreme effort. Then he set himself once more and heaved.

Something cracked. He screamed with the blinding pain. The darkness burst like a black star in his head.

When he came to again, he blinked at the pooling gold of twilight. Dusk already flitted like a gray moth in the shadowed recesses of the gorge. Fever sizzled at the back of his brain. Soon it would engulf him in a tossing, twitching helplessness.

He dredged up the shreds of raveled will that remained to him, sat up slowly and levered his leg free of the rocks. His fingers probed the swollen flesh. Yes ... the bone was in place. But he had to work fast, while there was still light enough and before the fever took him fully.

Noosing a strip of buckskin loosely around the leg, he set the six sticks in place beneath it and pulled the noose tight, cinching them down. He reinforced the makeshift splints with the remaining leather strips, tying each as tight as he could stand it.

When he was through, Will-Joe was almost too spent to move any more. But he did. He floundered his pain-wracked way back to Bloodgood's body. The jughead horse was quivering all over, raising its head in a last convulsive thrust. Its eyes seemed to question him.

My brother, his eyes said back, I was not thinking; I am sorry. It was as if a fellow creature had spoken and he spoke back: it was that natural.

He opened the large parfleche bag slung from Bloodgood's belt. His pistol and knife were inside. He cocked the pistol, jammed it behind the jughead's ear and pulled the trigger.

Thunderclap echoes slammed between the walls and died.

His throat flamed with a torturing thirst. He fumbled for Bloodgood's canteen. A large canteen almost full; the mountain man had filled it from the spring at Will-Joe's camp. With failing fingers he uncapped it and drank. He had hardly taken a swallow before the fever rolled like a redhot wheel across his senses. He set the canteen carefully aside and sank onto his back, giving himself utterly to the onset of delirium . . .

*　　*　　*

Three days passed. The fever came and went

like a bony ghoul, feeding on his body with each siege, leaving him a little weaker than before. Between visitations he forced himself to sluggish action, harnessing his weakening will and body to do what must be done to nurse and nourish the chemistry of life. Crawling on his belly a few inches at a time, he harvested edible roots and leaves from the scanty vegetation that grew within a short perimeter; he gathered every stray fragment of brush he could find. The smallest effort was a Herculean endeavor, and what would take a whole man only casual seconds to accomplish cost him eternities of grueling strain.

The immediate area was dry as a bone. Will-Joe conserved the water in the canteen with a miserly will. Bloodgood's parfleche contained a small quantity of jerky and a small loaf of pemmican. His jaws were too weak to masticate the jerky, but the tender parts of plants and the dried roasted fine-pounded meat of the pemmican went down easily. A sip of water to moisten his throat tissues, then a forced convulsive swallowing, enabled him to ingest tiny mouthfuls. One at a time, spaced well apart so that they would stay down.

He could not prevent his body water from sweating out during periods of fever-thrashing delirium, and so the water level in the canteen dropped at an alarming rate. The sun blistering all day into the gorge, caroming off its rocky walls and floor with a glaring fury, made the place like an oven. All he could do was stay in the meager shade of one wall or the other.

The effect of the intense heat became more unbearable with each passing day, and he could do nothing about it. Except to expend precious strength moving himself and a few necessities farther down the gorge. He had none to spare for the task of piling dirt and rocks over the bloating bodies of two horses and a man . . .

His leg was festering. It got worse daily. The inner flesh had been savagely macerated by torn bone: it swelled constantly outward against the sticks and buckskin lashings which had to be loosened and rebound each day to accommodate the fierce pressure. The pain of shattered bone was eclipsed by the pain of corruption; fear of a crooked leg was supplanted by the realization that he might lose the leg altogether. Assuming he could escape the cul-de-sac in time to find someone to take it off. But amputation, so far as he was concerned, was out of the question.

For the moment, so was escape. The sides of the gorge were unscalable, on this end at least, for they had fallen within sight of its south terminus which he could see boxed off cleanly. Its northward cut bent out of sight about fifty yards beyond his present position. In this remote area there was little likelihood of his being found, unless by Ulring or his cohorts from Spurlock . . . if they were still on the hunt. And that was a possibility he meant to discourage at all costs.

So that when Will-Joe made the decision in which lay any hope of saving his leg and his life, he waited till after dark on the third day to build a small fire. Darkness would hide telltale smoke. The wood he had gathered during lucid intervals made a pitifully small heap. He lighted it with a match from an oilcloth-wrapped packet he had found among Bloodgood's effects, then undid some of the bindings on his leg, stretched it out before him and slowly turned the blade of Bloodgood's knife in the flames.

He plunged the blade into the black bloated flesh, twisting savagely, his blood raging with a pain that went beyond pain. Pulling the knife free, he kneaded the flesh with his fists, continuing till a gush of blood and pus subsided. He sank back, spent and trembling, and left the wound open to drain . . .

By morning his fever had cooled. He felt somewhat stronger, almost clearheaded. The wound was draining nicely and the swelling had gone down. He rested through part of the morning, keeping the wound washed and clean, switching away hordes of flies, and finding enough energy to peg an occasional stone at the gaunt-necked carrion birds that spiraled down to light on the rimrock. They had come before: more of them each day, and they were getting bolder.

Will-Joe lay back and stared through slitted

eyes at their ominous black forms. Filth of the sky, I am not for you. The epithet had no force; he knew they were nature's sanitation corps. But he was not for them. Not yet.

The stench from what had attracted them had grown so bad that now his head was clearer, he could no longer bear it. The little distance he had managed to maneuver himself down the gorge made little difference in the overpowering putridity. Neither did his dim horror of letting the buzzards have their way.

He felt strong enough to attempt moving on, to investigate possibilities farther down. He had exhausted the edible shrubs and all but a few ounces of rancid water. Water. Food. These were his paramount needs. And finding a way out of the gorge . . .

He had a faded bandanna that was fairly clean. He knotted it around the wound, ate the last mouthful of pemmican and took a small swallow of water. Bloodgood's parfleche, containing the two knives, his pistol, cartridges and a few likely odds and ends, he secured to his belt at the back, along with the canteen, his blanket and his lariat. He tied a thong to the stock of Bloodgood's Winchester and looped that around his neck.

Then he began to crawl down the gorge, using hands and elbows and his good leg. It took him an hour to reach the bend. All the while he was aware of the flappings and gabblings of the buzzards. At the bend, he rested a moment and looked back. They had mounded in a squirming black shroud on the gorge bottom.

He crawled on . . .

*   *   *

The gorge ran another hundred yards beyond the bend. It took him all afternoon to reach its end. This tip boxed off too, but less precipitously. And it slanted a bit more inward.

Will-Joe was not sure he could scale it under the double handicap of a broken leg and his weakened condition, even with the aid of his lariat, but it was his only chance. Days of being on the run and living off scanty forage had already worn him gaunt. He was a little stronger now, strong enough to chew up some of the jerky and force it down, but it hardly filled his belly, and he had to stretch out what little he had.

A few more days and he would be too weak to make the attempt. If he escaped from the gorge, he could find water. Berries and insects and edible bark too—anything that would keep him alive till his leg was healed.

He rested from his crawl and chewed the jerky and scanned the face of the short cliff that terminated the gorge. It was full of irregularities that would support a man's weight, and it looked solid enough.

A sharp rock projected from the wall about

twenty feet up. If he could flip a noose over that, maybe he could pull himself up to a narrow ledge below it. He tried, sitting up and making a half-dozen casts, but each one fell short. He was in too awkward a position to make more than the clumsiest of throws.

Will-Joe looked around. A stunted aspen with a forked trunk grew out of the rubble close to the wall. He crawled over to it and used Bloodgood's knife to hack through its knotty base. When it came down, he trimmed off the limbs and whacked off the branching arcs of trunk above the fork. Measuring with his eye, he cut off a piece of his rope and tied one end around the ankle of his broken leg. He passed the other end over his right shoulder and tied it under his left arm.

Then, with the aid of the wall and the forked pole, he maneuvered slowly upright. The rope held his foot several inches above the ground. With the pole crotched securely in his left armpit, he was able to stand. He took a small tentative step. Yes, and even walk a little. He did not like the wrenching pressure of the rope's pull on the broken bone, but if the splints held fast, he could take it for brief periods.

He had ample leverage now, but casting the rope was still awkward. He could use only one arm while the other braced the crutch, and he could not shift his body to the throw. After eight casts, he succeeded in tossing his noose over the projection.

Will-Joe began to climb. His arms felt weak as water. It was a matter of pulling himself upward a few inches at a time, then resting his weight on the foot of his good leg, hooking it into any available crevice or wedging it against sliverlike projections. The slight burden of his rifle, blanket, canteen and the crutch which he also thonged to his neck did not give him much trouble. Sweat soaked the remnants of his clothing; he was dimly surprised to know he had that much liquid left in him.

It was getting dark by the time Will-Joe reached the ledge. And he had twenty more feet to go. The ledge was so narrow he had to hug the wall—no room to make another cast. All he could do was reach as high as possible, slip the noose over a short spur of rock, pull himself up and repeat the procedure till he achieved the rim.

He toiled upward, gaining a few feet each hour. Full darkness brought the high country chill and he no longer felt his tired fingers; they were too numb. He forced them to their work, groping out holds for the rope and his foot. His brain screamed with fatigue. He had to rest longer at each stop, yet he dared not rest too long: hugging against cold rock deadened his body, and should his grips relax even a moment, he would fall.

The time came when his groping hand as high as it reached could find nothing but a smooth bulging expanse of rock. No projections, nothing to lend support to hand or rope. He was marooned . . . at least so far as he could tell.

How far was he below the rim? It was too dark to be sure of anything. Maybe moonrise would show him a way . . . if he could cling to his shallow holds till then.

Will-Joe lay against the cliffside and shivered, fighting to hold onto a shred of consciousness. The tortured strain of his body was relaxing into numbness—what he feared most.

The last drop of resolution had almost squeezed from him when the wash of moonsilver topped the high ridge and shed enough light to skyline the rimrock. He was close to it, he saw. But not close enough. It was two feet above the length of his arm. A stub of rock elbowed out below it, but still a foot higher than he could reach.

If he could get his noose over that.

He could hardly hold the rope. On the third try he dropped the loop over the stub and jerked it tight. It was the work of many minutes to pull himself as high as the stub. But now the rim curved inward and he could haul himself bodily, inch by inch, up and over it.

He lay face down for many minutes, almost insensible. Feeling trickled back to his loosened muscles; so did the chill of the bare rock. Will-Joe dragged himself to a sitting position and wrapped himself in his blanket, the sluggish reflex of instinct.

He no longer thought. Too spent to function, his body and brain settled into a cocoon of waiting. For morning. For warmth. For life-giving movement . . .

CHAPTER FIFTEEN

Today had been too warm for cooking inside, so Rainbow Girl was preparing a mutton stew in a ring of blackened stones in front of the hogan. As she sat on her heels slowly stirring it, she kept her eyes on the kettle and listened to the talk between her grandfather and *Tsi Tsosi*.

They were standing a little distance off, the white man holding his horse's reins and talking in English, Adakhai replying in Navajo. It must be a matter of combative pride between them, since each spoke the other's tongue. Like most of the younger Navajos, she knew something of the white man's language, but it was hard to follow such a conversation.

She watched them from the corners of her eyes.

'I told you before how it is, Grandpa,' Ulring said. 'You go hiding that kid or helping him, a whole lot of trouble is going to get unloaded right here.'

'I have heard you.' Adakhai's face was a

crusty mask. 'Another thing Yellow Hair said is that he will drive us away from here when his suns are not so short.'

'Well, now maybe we can forget I said that.' Ulring slapped his reins idly against his palm, almost smiling. 'You could make things a little easier for us both, John.'

'How can I do that?'

'Listen, that kid isn't one of yours any more. He went away from you a long time back. Why stick your neck out? All he's brought you is trouble.'

'He did not bring the trouble.'

'Don't get hard-nosed, now. Let's talk about it. All right, say I believe you, say you don't know where he is now. Give me a couple of your boys, your best trackers. All I want is for 'em to find him for me. Just lead me to him, that's all. Now that's not a lot for what I'm offering.'

'What do you offer?'

'Things have been sort of rough for you people, haven't they? They don't have to be.'

'What passes with you, Yellow Hair? Do you beg?'

'You don't see it.' The reins slapped down hard on *Tsi Tsosi's* palm. 'I'm not talking about any middle ground. You scratch my itch, I scratch yours. Or I see to it you're run out of the country. That's the choice. Make up your mind. Now.'

'Listen to what I say, Yellow Hair.' Adakhai

lifted a knobby-jointed hand from his robe and held it palm up, fingers spread. 'Do you know how many ways a man can die? The country is big, and *Tsi Tsosi* goes often alone. Maybe one day he will not come back. It would take only one man. One gun or one bow.'

'Listen—'

'No. You have spoken. Now hear an old man. My young men are my eyes, they are my hands. If I point a finger, their eyes turn as I direct. Their hands will show as many guns as I say. But it will take one. Only one.'

Rainbow Girl watched the blood fill Ulring's face. His blue winter eyes turned on her and she knew that he was thinking back to when he had struck her and understanding why, at last, Adakhai had found his courage.

'I get it, Grandpa,' he said softly. 'Jesus, but you siwash sons of bitches are going to regret this.'

He wheeled with a choppy driving step, swung into his saddle, turned his animal and sent it loping away. Adakhai stood as he was, looking after him.

Rainbow Girl wrapped a rag around her hand and lifted the simmering kettle by its bail and pulled it off the fire. Then she rose and walked to the hogan, opened the reed door and stooped inside.

Will-Joe Cantrell lay in his blankets close to the piñon log wall, his body half-raised. He was peering out through a chink between the logs and bark mats, and his hand resting at his side was fisted around his pistol.

'Could you hear?' she asked.

He lay back and gazed at the roof. 'Some of it. Enough.'

She knelt down beside him, palms pressed together between her knees. 'If he had come in here, you would have shot him.'

'Yes.'

'Maybe you could have shot him through that hole.'

'I thought of it.'

He sounded faintly irritated and she knew he did not want to talk about it. In his place, she thought, she would have shot *Tsi Tsosi*. At least she believed so. But it was not Jahzini's way. He had a personal feeling about his fight with the white man. Maybe his white teacher had taught him to feel in that way. They were a strange people, the *Belinkana*. She thought she knew Jahzini, but he was part white too and maybe his white teaching woman understood him better. She gazed at his face, troubled, trying to read his thoughts, wondering.

He looked bony and wasted in the fresh calico shirt he wore, one of Adakhai's. His hands resting on the blanket that covered his legs were like brown claws. She knew that his body was lacerated with half-healed cuts and welts. It was a miracle that he had made it all this way, crawling sometimes, at other times hobbling on a forked pole with his broken leg held off the ground. It had taken him nearly a week. And he had been more dead than alive when he had stumbled into the village two nights ago.

Adakhai entered the hogan and scraped the door shut behind him.

'It is lucky he did not come with men,' he said. 'This time it was to ask a favor.'

Jahzini stirred his head. 'I heard.'

'Next time it will be with the men.'

Rainbow Girl said, 'I will look at the leg now.' She lifted the blanket and loosened the splints on Jahzini's leg, cleaning off the poultice she had put on. She ran a finger along the bone and felt the ridge where it had begun to knit cleanly. It was a wonder, considering what he had put the leg through.

Adakhai settled on his haunches, his eyes half-shuttered like a wrinkled lizard's. 'Do you think, Jahzini, he has found the old man he sent after you?'

'I don't think so. You know the place. Nobody goes there. But it has been a long time since Bloodgood went looking for me and maybe he thinks something has gone wrong. That's why he came today. It would be a thing like that, to make him ask your help.'

'*Juthla hago ni,*' muttered Adakhai. 'You must be gone from here, *shiyaazh*, before he comes again.'

'I've thought of this. I must leave these mountains.' Jahzini's voice was heavy. 'I bring you more trouble. There's no other way.'

'The *Belinkana* always mean trouble. I think of

206

you. Your leg needs time before you move again. We will move you—'

'There is a place,' Rainbow Girl said quickly. Both men looked at her. 'You know where it is, Jahzini.'

'Our cave.' He smiled a little. 'I remember how it was. A good place.'

'We will take you there,' Adakhai said. 'There are still his two men watching, so we will take you by night.' He rubbed his belly. 'Where is the food you made, Granddaughter?'

Rainbow Girl went out to get the kettle of stewed mutton. Billy Hosteen was standing a little way off, staring at the hogan. He looked at her as if he would say something. Abruptly he turned and walked away.

*   *   *

Ulring rode into the livery runway and swung slowly off his sorrel. It was dark and the place was deserted, the dim lantern burning. For a moment he stood leaning against his horse, one hand on the saddle leather, the other clenched so tight over the horn that the veins popped. Christ, he thought. Christ, take it easy.

He straightened. 'Claude!'

A solemn brown-faced boy descended a ladder from the loft. He stood rubbing one fist in his eyes, gazing sleepily at Ulring. 'I am Gregorio, señor. You want the horse put up?'

Ulring stared at him. Rodriguez, the owner's

oldest boy. Sure. What in hell had he been thinking of? Claude, Jesus. He had seen Claude buried two weeks ago.

'You're goddam right I want him put up. And snap your ass into it.'

The boy dropped his hand. 'Yes sir, Mister.'

Ulring strode out. A flame of temper scoured his thoughts black and ugly. *Goddam!* Was he losing his grip on everything? That dirty old bundle of bones John Thunder . . . he had gotten something in his belly besides corn liquor. Begging—he had come close to it, asking the old bastard for help. Christ, just wait till the other business was wrapped up and he could get a bunch of men up there. He would hit those stinking siwashes so fast and hard there wouldn't be any alive to reach the county line.

Something had happened to Bloodgood. Must have. If there was a white man in these parts who could find that kid, it was Bloodgood. That he hadn't come for the rest of his money could only mean one thing.

Ulring felt like a man holding the short end of nothing. Failure was the dirtiest word in his lexicon. Getting that kid had come to obsess him as no goal ever had, even Bethany. By now it had gone far beyond any peripheral danger the kid might pose; it was the failure that festered like a worsening gallsore.

He headed for the Pink Lady. Get the Navajo stink out of his mouth with a drink, maybe he could think again. But his steps

208

slowed. He saw the warm-squared light that was the front window of the McAllister home. Stared at it and felt his anger fed. She could not turn her back on him, by God, if that was what she thought, not in Frank Ulring's own town.

He paused outside the house. The blinds were pulled, but he saw her shadow move across one. Well, by God. He went up the path and rapped on the door.

She opened it part way. 'Good evening, Frank. I'm a little busy . . .'

'I know. You've been busy close on two weeks.'

He stood staring at her, ready, so help him, to ram his foot in the door if she tried to close it. She was out of mourning—he noticed that at once—wearing a tidy blue-and-white-checked gingham, the lamp behind her building her hair to a shimmering corona. Desire and frustration jolted him like a fist.

'I've called on you three times and it's the same thing . . . "I'm busy, Frank." One night it's preparation for tomorrow, school stuff. Another time you're getting ready for bed. Or else you're just plain tired. Well, I'm getting a little tired too, lady.'

She stood a moment, her face composed as a madonna's. Then gave a little resigned twitch of her shoulders and said 'Come in,' opening the door, stepping aside, closing it behind him.

Ulring paused in the act of pulling off his hat. He saw the two open trunks on the *sala*

209

floor, one already stuffed lid-high with household articles. He must have interrupted her packing of the other. It was half-filled with clothes, and she had other clothes laid out, draped over the sofa and chairs. He swept his hat in a slow quarter-circle.

'Now what's all this?'

'I'm packing my things.'

She picked up a dress and began to fold it. He looked at the stuff again. This was no visit she was going on, not with everything but the kitchen stove in tow.

'Beth—' He tried an indulgent chuckle. 'Now listen, what is this? Are you thinking of leaving us?'

'Not thinking, Frank.' She raised her eyes. 'I am leaving. For good and all. I'm going back to Boston.'

'But this is your home. Everything . . .'

'Is being packed, as you can see. Mr Rodriguez will put up the house for sale and send me the money when it's sold.'

'That greaser? You expect him to . . .'

He let the words trail. There was a look in her face he had never seen. Not hatred—quite. Loathing perhaps. Or pity.

'That's very typical, Frank. But I should know by now who my friends are. I think I do.'

She bent back to her work. Ulring gazed at her, swaying a little. His hat crushed to a damp ball in his fist at his side.

'Why, Beth? Can you tell me why?'

'All my living ties are in Boston. Why not? I have nothing here.'

'There's the school.'

'Summer vacation begins shortly. The town can bring in another teacher by fall.'

'All *right*!' He set his hands on the back of a chair and leaned across it. 'What about us, then? You and me?'

'What about us, Frank? I don't recall any understanding between us, do you?'

Silence ticked in his head like a clock. The small rustlings as she packed the trunk rasped his nerves like miniature files. Finally he said raggedly:

'That night. The time Claude was killed. The kid was here, wasn't he? Came to see you. He talked to you.'

'Yes, we talked.'

'You believed him. Goddam it, didn't you? Took that killer's word over mine.'

'Tell me something, Frank—' She picked up another dress and shook it out. 'Why did you tell those men to shoot to kill, after you'd given me your promise to take Will-Joe alive?'

'I wanted to spare you, that's why.' He could be facile in this, having prepared an answer long ago. 'It was a bad promise, I admit it. That kid is a rattlesnake. I knew it even if you didn't. And I was damned if I was going to risk the lives of good men taking him. Decent men . . . you know them. Didn't they deserve that much edge over a thieving, murdering breed?'

A little smile tweaked the corners of her lips; she shook her head very slightly.

'What does that mean?'

'That I won't argue with you. Think what you please. You always did.'

'No argument, eh? No more pretty excuses. No horse manure about the pore little Injun bastard we all helped make what he is.'

'Well, I'd imagine you can recite it all for yourself now, Frank. Like a poem out of *McGuffey's*.'

He stared at her, feeling the raw heat stream from his brain through his whole body, desiring her in this moment of losing her as he never had before, seeing how lamplight made ivory of her flesh and limned with deep shadow the underswells of two breasts that were large and lovely, firm as ripe fruits. The fantasy he had entertained many times shook him with a fanged fury, peeling away demure gingham and dainty camisole, revealing her naked and bedded, red-gold hair fanned like flame on a white pillow, all her beauty pulsing only for him.

'Yeah . . . never had a chance.' He stared; a muscle jerked in his cheek. 'A man makes his chances. I always said so.'

'Frank . . .' Her eyes moved across his face. 'I think you'd better leave.'

'Not tonight.'

The chair was between them. His hands tightened and flung it aside. He caught her by the shoulders and saw her eyes dilate and her mouth open. *'Don't scream, Beth!'* He jammed his hand over her mouth and his arm snaked around her waist like a cable, crushing her against him. With his face inches from hers, he said:

'Now you hear me. You're not dumb. You know what I waited for two years ... what I wanted. You wanted it too. I saw it like reading a book. Now you wanted it right, didn't you, all legal with ribbons on it? Sure. So did I. That miserable worthless pipsqueak, what was he, what good was he to anyone, least of all you? That's what I cut out of your life, like you cut off a gangrene foot.' He raised his hand a quarter-inch from her mouth. 'You ought to see that, what I really did, why I did it.'

'You're hurting me.'

Slowly, very slowly, he let go of her and she backed away a few steps. He followed her, keeping close, ready to grab her again if she tried to scream.

'I see it, Frank.' Her head moved from side to side, and he saw she was afraid now. 'But you don't. Oh God, you don't see it at all.'

'What?' He put out his hand but stopped it short of her, his eyes stark as a wolf's, shaking with lust. 'What don't I?'

'Everything—'

Her eyes were inured to him. Repudiation. Loss. It howled in his mind.

His hand reached and seized and tore,

213

ripping gingham. Pearly flesh shone and his eyes moved and softened and gently his hand moved, caressing, not holding. God, more beauty than he had dreamed, he could be tender, just let her be—

The shrinking ripple of her flesh was communicated to his dreamily exploring hand. Instinct shot the hand up to lock her throat and throttled her scream on the first note. He shook her. Bitch. Strumpet. Whore. Good enough for the fondlings of a green-gutted worm like McAllister, but not for Ulring, eh? Your white flesh is an abomination and by whatever God no man will touch it, not when I've done—

His hand became a vise. Her eyes glazed. Her fingers taloned on his hand and furrowed downward. Pain splintered his fury. He swung her and let go and she was flung away, crashing against the wall.

She hung there, her throat working soundlessly. Her eyes cleared but the expression in them did not change. Bitch. Harlot. He tramped toward her, shoulders up, his arms hanging. He reached again, both hands now lifting to her throat—

Through the red haze he dimly knew that her right hand was moving, coming up past his sliver of awareness so that the elbow he raised to block it was too late. Something shattered against his head like a bomb.

All went black for an instant. Then he was on

his knees, waggling his head from side to side, hands clasped over his ringing ears. Feet running, a door slamming open, running again and then silence. Christ Jesus. He gazed down, holding his head. Broken bits of a glass chimney, the reek of coal oil. She had scooped a dead lamp off the table by the wall and swept it up at his head. What had hit him? The lamp's weighted base, that was it. Christ. He was bleeding over the ear. He looked at the bright smear on his palm with a vague feeling of surprise.

Ulring staggered to his feet, leaning against the wall with his head down. The whirling floor steadied. All right, bitch, where are you? He remembered the sound of running. Ah, kitchen. Back way. Swaying uncertainly, he moved through the darkened house and stopped at the kitchen door. It hung wide open.

He blinked at the night. 'Beth,' he said gently.

He stood there a full minute, then tramped back to the *sala*. He stared broodingly at the trunks. His rioting tendrils of thought knotted back to a kernel of wet fury.

He seized hold of the trunk of household goods, veins squirming in his temples as he strained it up and heaved it over. He kicked and stomped, crushing pans, smashing crockery, demolishing glassware. But his attention veered almost at once to the other trunk. Clothes. Hers. Things of daintiness,

215

intimacy, night-things. He fingered a nightgown, pale thing of smoke and cobweb, then made fists and yanked them savagely apart till the gown hung in two shreds. He went through the trunk, pitching everything on the floor, tearing and trampling as he went. His spurs hooked in a delicate swirl of silk; he kicked and it tore like paper.

The destruction pleased him. His brain went cold again. He picked up his hat and walked to the door and paused. He looked on his work and was satisfied.

'You'll have a pretty hope chest for the devil, sweetheart.'

He laughed and tramped out.

CHAPTER SIXTEEN

The back yard was unkept, overgrown with rioting weeds and brush. Bethany had hidden herself in a tangle of shrubbery, flattening her body down on the dew-soaked ground. She heard Frank come to the back door and softly call her name. After a minute his footsteps retreated. The sound of things being smashed reached her faintly. Then the front door slammed. Maybe he was gone, but she did not know, so she lay for a long time, not daring to move in spite of the wet chill of the ground.

Finally, unsteadily, she got up and moved to

216

the open door, listened for several minutes and then went inside. She knew where a gun was, a gun she had never touched. Dennis used to wear it in a shoulder holster under a frock coat—an affectation that had irritated her—and after most of their other possessions had been pawned, some illusion of manliness had made him hold onto the gun. She tiptoed down a corridor to the dark bedroom, opened the commode drawer that still held Dennis's things and located the gun by feel. She saw it in her mind: a small one-shot British pistol that Dennis had always kept loaded.

It felt strange in her hand. Always she had deemed herself so secure; thoughts of prowlers had never troubled her. After tonight, she wondered, would she ever feel secure again?

Bethany went out to the *sala*. She gazed at the carnage, the ruin of cherished things, with sickened eyes. Slowly then, her back straightened. She went to the door, shot the inside bolt into place, returned to the kichen and locked that door too. Then, in her bedroom, she lighted the lamp on the commode and looked at herself in the Adamesque mirror mounted on the armoire.

Was that her? Dear God. Bodice and camisole hanging in shreds, hair in straggles, skin and clothes smudged with moist earth, great bruises on her bare arms. She arched her neck, wincing at its soreness. It wore the mottled prints of Ulring's fingers. He is crazy.

Her lips formed the words, but only a croaking whisper came from her bruised throat.

Fool, she thought bitterly. Brave? There was no virtue in stupidity. Trying to be so cocksure, coolly admitting the man she was sure had killed Dennis, letting him see her preparations to leave. All that would be necessary should he get out of hand (she hadn't dreamed he would dare) would be a single piercing scream. Neighbors would hear, friends would come. She had frighteningly underestimated the bull-fierce fury that could crush a woman's fragile self-assurance like a straw.

Insane . . .? No. Too easy a gauge. It was deeper. Soul-deep. The callous evil in the man went beyond crazed whim or ruthless resolution. He was immune to decency. Had to be, to have calculated so long and patiently, to execute so deliberately. Qualms? Misgivings? She doubted he had ever felt them. He was a man who simply wanted . . . and took.

Bethany began to tremble; her lips quivered. She bit her lip, determined not to cry. But she could not stop the wild trembling. She remembered, miracle of miracles, that Dennis had left a quarter-full bottle among his effects. Whiskey. God, she hated it. She had reason to. But anything . . .

She poured a drink and took it, coughing and shuddering. She filled the wash basin and wet a cloth and wiped the smudges from her face, feeling the liquor glow warm her. What should she do? Leave tomorrow on the stage as she had intended?

She felt the whalebone spirit of her puritan blood tighten her spine. Why should she run ... from Frank or from anything? It wasn't in her nature. Never had been. She had hated the itinerant years with Dennis, but not to have joined his runnings would have meant another sort of running—from her duty, from herself.

She must do something to bring Dennis's killer to justice. She could tell friends what had happened ... tell them the whole story. They would believe her, but would it be enough? They could protect her from Ulring. They could even arrest him. But at considerable risk, for Frank was a dangerous man and would be doubly so if he were cornered.

Even if they took him, it would be for nothing. There was simply no proof that he'd killed Dennis. Nothing but the word of a half-breed boy.

Would that be enough? Not before, she thought, but maybe now, backed by her own story, it would be. It was a chance, but it had to be taken. Certainly Will-Joe would be no worse off. Sooner or later, so long as he stubbornly refused to leave the region, he was bound to be captured or killed.

She had to find Will-Joe. But how?

The Navajos. If anybody knew his whereabouts, they did.

Tomorrow, she thought. She knew where the

219

village was; she had been there once, in a fruitless effort to enlist some of the children in her school. Old John Thunder had been polite but disinterested.

This time he would listen. He had to.

*   *   *

Squatting on his heels behind a screen of brush, Billy Hosteen watched a pair of young girls saunter down the path to the spring. He was a hundred feet away and could watch them unobserved. He wore a fixed frown and broke small twigs between his fingers, listening to their chatter and laughter while they took their time filling their skin waterbags.

Where was she? Always, at this time of day, she came for water. He had waited for her many times before the sharp words had passed between them. But it had been a long time since they had spoken, and he could no longer quiet the bitter festering in him. He must talk to her. He hoped that she would be along soon. And that these clucking children would be gone before she came.

Finally they had filled their waterbags and were returning up the path. As they passed out of sight, he heard them speak Rainbow Girl's name. Then he heard her voice. They had met her in the path and the three of them chatted for a minute, the two girls teasing her. Jahzini, they said, was a catcher of horses; it would take her a long time to water so many horses.

Billy ground his teeth. Everyone knew that she meant to go daily to Jahzini's hiding place, taking him food. No doubt, as such things went, when he was well enough, he would tie his horses before Adakhai's hogan in the way of any courting youth. No doubt too, Rainbow Girl would water them to signify her acceptance.

Billy Hosteen's thoughts were dark and bitter. Long ago he should have brought his horses to her lodge. But he had never been sure of her. She had a grave gentle way of holding him at arm's length so that he was never sure of her feelings. And then Jahzini had returned and he had sensed at once that he had lost all favor in her eyes. Even as a child, he remembered, her eyes had been for Jahzini alone. They had been children together and their attachments as they played their childish games had been warm. Jahzini had been his friend, and nothing else had mattered. But they were no longer children.

The talk broke off and Rainbow Girl came into view on the path, smiling a little as she descended into the brush-enclosed swale where the spring lay. She knelt and dipped her waterbag. Billy Hosteen rose and walked to the spring. She looked up once, then lowered her gaze to the water. He stopped a few yards away.

'*Ahalani*, Rainbow Girl.'

'*Ahalani*, Narbona.'

He sat down on his haunches and picked up a handful of sand, sifting it through his fingers as he watched her. 'In three suns,' he said tentatively, 'I go to work breaking horses for the white-eyed rancher Johnson.'

'You have worked for him before.'

'Yes, but I only cut hay for him. Now he will pay me for each horse I break. I will make more than the white-eyes who take care of his cattle.'

'That will please your father.'

'I do not care about that.' Anger rose in his voice; he tried to suppress it. 'Soon I can buy whatever I want. If I had a woman, she would have finer things than any other Navajo.'

'Perhaps that would please her, then.'

'Please her. Of course it would.'

'If she cared about such things, of course.'

Her voice remained solemn and pleasant and quite indifferent. He ground his teeth in a quiet fury. She rose to her feet, holding the filled waterbag, round and darkly glistening now, in front of her.

'Narbona,' she said quietly, 'sometimes two things are said where only one is meant. Often we do this. But sometimes it is not a good thing. There are others who would be happy if Narbona's ponies were tied before their hogans.'

He stood up too. Saying the words thickened his throat. 'You would never water them.'

'There are others, Narbona.'

She turned away and he moved quickly and caught her sleeve. She looked at him and he let his hand drop.

'It is Jahzini. Why?'

'How can I answer that? There is a difference.'

'Yes,' he said thickly. 'He wears a *Belinkana* name.'

'So do you, when you go among them.'

'But I am not part white-eyes. I think that that is it.'

'No. It's you who would like to be white-eyes, Narbona. You who think their ways so fine that you want the things they have. You would live among them as an equal if they would let you. Because you want this, you think that others do.'

Her stare was straight as an arrow. It made him uncomfortable.

'Then what is the difference?'

'You are not Jahzini. That is the difference.'

She turned her back and headed up the path. Rage clotted his brain. He opened and closed his fists. *Jahzini*. If not for him . . .

He knew what he would do. Now.

It had been in his mind before. He had been thinking of it since this morning when he had followed her to the place above the racing water where the cave was. He could do the thing safely; none of The People would know how it was done. Yet he had hesitated.

Now it would be easy to do.

223

A little later, jogging down the trail toward the Winnetka basin, he felt less sure.

Tsi Tsosi ... Yellow Hair. Just the name made a dryness in Billy Hosteen's throat. He remembered too well the time that the sheriff had caught up with his brothers and him after they had run off cows from a valley ranch and how he had narrowly escaped. How Ulring had coolly shot both his brothers through the head and left their bodies for the Navajos to find. For a time Billy had lived in the fear that Yellow Hair would come looking for him. But he never did. He had made his point.

Still, Billy Hosteen had more reason than any Navajo to fear the sheriff. He tried to reason it away: *Tsi Tsosi* would listen to one who could lead him to Jahzini. And afterward be in his debt ... or at least consider the old score suitably evened. Thinking about it did little to ease the knot of drying phlegm in Billy's throat. But he thought of Jahzini too. And Rainbow Girl. Which made it easier to think about the other ...

Rousing with a start, he reined up his horse. What was that? Someone coming up the trail. Tall pines mantled the south slope of the ridge he was crossing; he could not see the rider below, but he identified a muffled thud of hoofs on needle detritus. A stab of guilty reflex, and not a well-grounded reason, made him pull his horse offside into the timber. He did not want to be seen by whoever it was ... not just now.

Soon he saw the rider coming through the trees. A *Belinkana* woman riding sidesaddle. Slits of sunfire rippling across her moving form turned her hair to quiet flame. It was the teaching woman from Spurlock. In a minute she had passed out of sight.

Puzzled, he turned his mount back down the trail. Why was she riding toward the Navajo town? Could it have anything to do with Jahzini? Billy Hosteen did not know, but he urged his horse on a little faster . . .

CHAPTER SEVENTEEN

The Winnetka ran wide and shallow at its upper stem, but as it cut through this arm of rugged foothills it roiled turbulently between the rocky narrows. Here and there its brawling current broadened out shallowly again; at its most tumultuous, the Winnetka was more a large creek than a true river. At these places the boulder-strewn banks pulled back against the tall bony ridges that flanked the stream for miles along its lower run. If a man were high enough on a ridge, he had a picturesque and rather panoramic view of the rivercourse. Little timber other than the usual scrub evergreens and a few dwarf aspens. But the rock strata exposed by age-old erosion of the dropping streambed was pleasant to look at, especially when sunrise and sunset turned the salt and iron in the rock to a slapdash painter's palette of glowing colors.

Will-Joe, however, had gazed on the scene for a day and a half. This morning, sitting in the cave mouth with his torso propped up by a willow-weave backrest and his splinted leg out straight before him, he wished he had something to read. He liked to read in the winters when there wasn't much to do. He used to borrow from Miss Bethany's library, particularly Scott's romances. He wished he had *Kenilworth* or *Ivanhoe*. Worlds of pageantry, knighthood, strange Anglo-Saxon customs that he knew had shaped half his heritage.

As it was, all he did was sit in the cave opening and stare out and think. He was tired of thinking; his thoughts spun in circles back to their starting points.

The Navajos had brought him here on a horse drag after dark two nights ago, afterward taking pains to obliterate the trail. Rainbow Girl had come the next day. She brought cooked food so he wouldn't have to risk a fire and she changed the dressings on his leg. They had talked a lot, and he looked forward to her visits. More for her company than for the particular delicacies that she prepared with great care, remembering how he liked them.

He thought about her now, lazy satisfying thoughts, and about what he might do after his

226

leg had healed. He still wasn't sure. He thought of Bloodgood, for whose death he would be blamed if the remains were ever found. He almost smiled at that: how many killings could they hang you for?

The cave was cool and roomy with a roughly arched ceiling and a sandy floor but an opening so low and tight that it couldn't be spotted from below. Even seated in the mouth, he was sheltered by jaws of rock to either side, shaded by an overhang above. Yet he could see a good way up and down the river gorge.

He had felt wary at first, less from fear that any Navajo would betray him than that Rainbow Girl's comings and goings might be spotted; she might be trailed. But yesterday she had told him that at last, out of disgust or boredom, the two white-eyes had broken off their long vigil above the lodges and left.

Will-Joe yawned and lay back, half-shutting his eyes. He scratched the pleasant itch in his knitting leg. Finally he dozed.

A brittle sound of horses' hoofs brought him sharply awake. He lay very still for a moment, his heart pounding.

He should have seen whoever was coming, but by now they were at the base of the ridge, cut off from his view by shelving rock. Two horses, he thought, one of them shod. Now they were halting. He palmed up his pistol from his side. And waited. It was all he could do.

He heard the riders slowly ascend the steep

flank of the ridge, nearing the cave. Then Rainbow Girl's soft voice: 'Jahzini!' He answered, feeling a flood of relief.

A moment later she climbed up past the rock shelf, and behind her came Miss Bethany. He stared. He could hardly believe it, even when she knelt by his side and took his hand. She was wearing a green riding habit with a fancily draped skirt, wrinkled as if she had slept in it, a ridiculous little hat perched on her red-gold hair. Her smooth and cool touch made his heart slug in his throat; he had difficulty finding words:

'How did you get here?'

'Not too hard . . . with a good guide.'

She smiled at Rainbow Girl who was on her knees opening a parfleche bag she had brought. She did not look up. Will-Joe felt a small embarrassment. He said in the Navajo tongue: 'You should not have brought her.'

'I thought you would want to see her.' Rainbow Girl's voice was very flat. 'She came yesterday to the lodges. She told *Natani* that she would see you, but his face was closed to her. I told her if it was her wish, I would make a place for her in our hogan and in the morning I would bring her here. I thought this would be your wish too.'

He didn't know what to say. Miss Bethany looked from one of them to the other, then said: 'Is something wrong?'

'No, ma'am. I only wondered why you came.'

'Something happened . . . I think it changes the situation.'

She talked. He listened carefully to her words, noticing the dark bruises on her neck above the lacy throat ruffles of her jacket. Anger blazed him. Ulring. He had done this— he had dared to hurt her. I could have killed him, he thought. Many times while he looked for me I could have waited for him.

He had felt the same when Adakhai had told him that Rainbow Girl had saved his life by knocking up the sheriff's rifle and that Ulring had struck her. Remembering that too, he wished more than ever that he had killed the white-eyes when there had been the chance.

'Will-Joe . . . you said once that you would be willing to stand trial. Are you still willing?'

'Why?'

'Because now it's the way. Don't you see, with my story to back up yours . . .'

'He's still the law. Do I give myself up to him?'

'No. When your leg is better, I'll come again . . . with friends. We'll take you to Spurlock. There's a thing called citizen's arrest. We can arrest the sheriff and hold him in custody for the circuit judge. Then the law will decide. But not Frank Ulring's law . . . I promise you.'

He said nothing.

'What's the matter? Before, you—'

'That was before.' His voice was flat and emotionless. 'He has hunted me. Soon this leg

229

will be well. Then I will hunt him.'

'No . . . oh no! Why? If it's because of me—'

'And her.'

He looked at Rainbow Girl as he spoke. Her face lifted quickly; he met her eyes, wanting her to understand, knowing that she would.

Miss Bethany leaned forward. 'Listen to me. You always listened, at least.'

'Yes'm.'

'I told you how our judicial—how a court works.'

'Yes'm. Judicial system.'

She flushed. 'Then you know that what you propose is as much murder—'

'That man deserves to be killed. That is the difference.'

'In the eyes of the law, it's the same! And you'll be where you are now . . . hunted, a wanted killer. Don't you see, he will hang for what he's done, and it would be for nothing!'

'Are you so sure?' His eyes challenged her. 'When I said before the white man's law is for white men, you said yes. Now you will take the chance, eh? The breed's word against the white man's. And maybe the court doesn't listen, he goes free. There's the chance, eh?'

'Yes. I don't deny there's a chance . . . but can't you take it?'

'I have a sure way, I think.'

'I hoped for so much from you.' Her voice was hurt and bitter. 'I tried to teach you better ways . . . hoping that you might teach your

230

people.'

'Better ways? We have our ways too, Miss Bethany. But we are just savages.'

'I didn't say . . .'

'Maybe that is what they do then. When the *Belinkana* take our lands away. When they make the treaties they never keep. When they kill the buffalo so we will starve. When they rob us and lie to us and starve us, it is all right. They are teaching us better ways.'

'Don't.' She turned her face away. 'I am trying to save your life. Nothing else. If you can't see that . . .'

He felt a touch on his shoulder. He looked at Rainbow Girl; her eyes were shining strangely.

'She is right, Jahzini.'

'Do you know what we said?'

'Enough. She is not like the other *Belinkana*. It is not the same with her. Once you told me this, now I see. I think it is the way to do, the way she has said.'

*   *   *

'There it is,' Billy Hosteen said. 'Right above the horses.'

Ulring halted his horse and followed the Navajo's pointing arm. All he saw was a ridgeflank of tawny crumbling rock. 'You sure?'

'Sure. Like I said, you can't see nothing from down here. But it's right there, the cave.'

The soft roar of water covered their voices.

231

They had followed the Winnetka downstream for some distance, riding along its shallow, roiling, boulder-strewn bed. They were now about two hundred yards from the place that Billy Hosteen had indicated. Two horses stood at the base of the ridge, ground-tied. They had spotted the animals just as they'd come around a bend in the stream.

Ulring narrowly studied the scene. So Bethany was here. Maybe it was just as well.

His first reaction when Billy Hosteen had come to him late yesterday had been one of suspicion. He remembered the cattle-stealing incident of a few years back; the two Navajos he had killed had been this one's brothers. If any of John Thunder's Navajos had a reason for wanting to see Yellow Hair cash in his chips, it was him. He might have set something up with Cantrell. Ulring had warned Billy that he would ride behind him all the way: at the first sign of a trap, he was a dead man.

He was anyway, in Ulring's mind. No witnesses. Nobody to carry any more tales. Once Billy Hosteen had guided him to the places, his usefulness was ended. Two dead siwashes instead of one, that was all. The same for Bethany McAllister. He hated the idea, but Bethany knew too much: you never knew what her emancipated kind of woman might have cooking in that beautiful head.

He had decided as much right after Billy Hosteen had told him of passing the red-haired schoolteacher on his way to Spurlock. Ulring had checked at the livery barn. Yes, Gregorio the hostler had said, Miss Bethany had rented a horse—the lineback dun—and had said she might be gone for two or three days. She had not elaborated.

If she had been heading for the Navajo village, Ulring had guessed it was to find Cantrell. Bethany had changed her mind about leaving on the stage, that much was clear; now so was the fact that she was cooking up something with Cantrell. There was the lineback dun.

Well, by God.

'That other horse,' Ulring said. 'The paint. You know who owns him?'

'Sure, that's one of old John's string. Rainbow Girl, she rides him sometimes.'

Her too, Ulring thought. His lips peeled off his teeth—remembering how she had spoiled his aim when Cantrell had been dead in his sights. He didn't mind the thought at all . . .

'All right,' he said. 'Let's study what we'll do. You listening?'

Billy didn't move.

'What's the matter?'

'Well, I just say I lead you here.' Billy grinned with a kind of nervous swagger. 'I figure now you know where he is, I go home.'

'I figure you don't,' Ulring said. 'Reason you don't, I need someone to pull him out of the cave. Tell you what you do—'

'Look, please, mister. I done what I said.'

'Shut up.' Ulring rubbed his chin, staring at the stony ridge face. 'What you do, you ride up by those other horses and give a yell. When he comes out, your job's done.'

He reached down to the booted rifle under his knee and pulled it free. It was a Sharps Big Fifty, a buffalo gun. Billy Hosteen stared at it; oily sweat shone on his face.

'Listen, maybe he don't come out. His leg is broke. He got this kind of crutch he use. But I think maybe one of the women come out.'

'Maybe. He trust you?'

'I don't know. We used to be friends.' There was a plea in Billy's voice. 'Maybe he don't trust me no more. Maybe he think I try trap him.'

Ulring nodded thoughtfully. 'That's what I figure. So he won't let either woman show herself and maybe catch a bullet.'

'He don't come out himself neither then.'

Ulring smiled and patted the rifle. 'Well, boy, that's why you got to talk right up. Make big medicine, savvy? Tell him old Yellow Hair is up at the village with a bunch of white men raising six kinds of hell. Burning hogans, screwing all the squaws. You want the white schoolmarm to come see if she can call me off. I bet he comes out then. Allright? Now you move along; do like I said.'

He jabbed Billy Hosteen lightly in the chest with the Sharps, his eyes hard. Billy pulled his

234

horse back, opened his mouth as if to say something, closed it and put his horse into motion downstream.

Ulring dismounted in the ankle-deep water, swearing as his foot slipped on the slick-pebbled bed. He gave the reins a tug, pulling the sorrel over toward a massive block-shaped boulder that had once toppled down from the ridge. It completely sheltered them both.

Ulring pulled off his hat and leaned against the right flank of the boulder, lining his rifle barrel along the rock. Above it, only his eye and the side of his head showed. He could sight in nicely from here and the Sharps had an effective range of over five hundred yards. Fish in a barrel.

Billy Hosteen climbed his horse out of the waters up to a low bank where the ridge began to rise. He looked back once in Ulring's direction, then tipped his head up.

'Jahzini!' he called. 'Jahzini! *Nishtli* Narbona!'

CHAPTER EIGHTEEN

'It is Narbona,' Will-Joe said.

The three of them had heard the rider pull up below. For a moment they had waited tensely. Now, hearing Billy Hosteen's voice, Will-Joe reached for his crutch. Rainbow Girl laid a hand on his arm.

'Wait. I will go out.'

'Why?' His eyes searched her face. 'You do not trust Narbona?'

She hesitated. 'I don't know. It is not easy to say . . . he wanted to tie his ponies before *Natani's* lodge. He told me this.'

'What did you tell him?'

'That there were other lodges.'

Will-Joe thought about it, remembering Narbona's bitterness. You can't be sure of anything, he thought, but it is nothing to take a chance on. Anyone who stepped on the shelving rock beyond the cave mouth would be partly exposed.

'Don't go out,' he told Rainbow Girl. And raised his voice: *'Ha'at iisha?'*

'It is important,' Billy Hosteen called back. 'Come out . . . I will tell you.'

'I hear you well. Say what it is.'

'It's Yellow Hair. He came to the lodges with many white-eyes. Adakhai sent me. The white teaching woman must come and talk to Yellow Hair. Maybe he will leave us alone.'

Will-Joe lowered his body till he was stretched on his belly. Then he went at a slow crawl across the cave floor toward the open shelf.

'What are you doing?' Rainbow Girl whispered.

'Be still . . . wait.'

He inched across the shelf till his eyes just

236

cleared the rim. Flat on his belly, he had a wide view up and down the river gorge without showing himself. There was Billy Hosteen below him. Alone. Still not satisfied, Will-Joe took in the scene piece by piece, weighing every detail.

'I see you, Jahzini. Why do you hide on your belly?'

That was Billy Hosteen mocking him, but the voice wore a frantic edge. Will-Joe took his time. He had been staring at this landscape for two days: If anything was awry, he would find it.

Something was down there. Something that hadn't been. A barely discernible lump at the edge of a boulder. He gazed at it till he was sure. A man was behind that rock.

He laughed. 'Narbona. Tell Yellow Hair to go home. Then I will stand up.'

Billy Hosteen's nerve broke. He turned his horse and kicked him into a run, streaking up the gorge.

The shot sent echoes caroming between the ridges. The bullet smashed Billy off his horse like a broken doll. He hit the rushing water face-down and was motionless, his clothes turning dark in the shallow current.

Keeping flat down, Will-Joe slithered backward into the cave. He reached for his crutch, and Rainbow Girl helped him stand. He looped the rope over his chest to hold his leg off the ground, then looked at Miss Bethany, her white hand clasped at her throat. All the color had left her face.

'The sheriff is here, ma'am. Billy Hosteen brought him. Now Billy is dead.'

'A . . . trap?'

'It didn't work. So he shot Billy. He does not want any witnesses. Now I think he will try to get above us. We have no chance here. I will have to get up there first.'

'No, Jahzini!' Rainbow Girl picked up Bloodgood's Winchester, holding it away from him. 'Your leg . . . I will go up.'

He took a lurching step forward, grabbed hold of the rifle and wrenched it from her hands.

'You will stay, both of you. Here.' He thrust his pistol into Rainbow Girl's hand. 'Whatever happens, whatever you hear . . . don't come out unless I tell you.'

He crutched slowly out of the cave and stopped just outside. Hidden by a flanking wing of rock, he could still scan the gorge. The dark lump along the boulder was gone . . . but Ulring's big sorrel stood in the stream, reins trailing.

He was sure he had guessed right. Ulring had fallen back behind the bend, and now he would come up on the ridge from that side.

Unless it was a trick. Unless he was still behind the boulder.

One way to find out. Only one, Will-Joe thought. And stepped out into view, watching the boulder. Ready to drop flat at the hint of a movement.

Nothing happened, not right away. And he could not wait any longer: once Ulring scaled the ridge and got above them, they were trapped. He might even start rolling rocks to bury them in the cave.

The rawhide sling was still on his rifle. He looped it around his neck and began to climb up past the cave, using his hands as much as he could. The slope was treacherously steep, a jumble of shattered rock and sliding rubble. Even a man with two good legs wouldn't scale its three hundred or so feet in a couple of minutes. It grew steeper as he went higher. He was forced to stop, hang the crutch around his neck by the attached thong, and tackle the rest of the ascent at a crawl. His useless leg bumped and jarred. He set his teeth against the pain, sweating and straining himself upward with his hands and bracing himself all he could with his good leg.

Finally he stopped. He was sweat-drenched, fatigued, trembling all over. He still had a hundred feet to go, but he had to rest.

He caught a sound of boots rasping across rock. Ulring was holding back off the rim out of sight as he moved this way along the ridgetop.

Was he this close already? It hit Will-Joe with a jolting despair. He quickly unslung his rifle. Ulring would be above him in a moment. He had to find cover fast. Above him was a flat pocket grooved deep into the ridgeside; chunks of rock littered it. One might shelter him, though he doubted it. Ulring, able to shoot down, would have the advantage.

He climbed doggedly toward the pocket. Had nearly reached it when a stone under his foot plowed away. He let go of his rifle, clawing with both hands at the slick rock. The rifle slid downward, clattering across the slanting rubble till it stopped in a crevice a hundred feet below.

He pulled himself up to the ledge and fell exhaustedly on his face. Disarmed and helpless . . . he might as well wait for it. But an angry flare of desperation drove him to heave over on his belly.

He unslung the crutch. Began to push up to his feet.

Then he glanced downslope. His throat thickened. Rainbow Girl had left the cave. She must have heard the rifle fall. She started quickly upward, slim form dark against the crumbled yellow rock.

'Go back!' It tore out of him in a hoarse yell. 'Go back!'

She ignored him. Reached the rifle and scooped it up, then continued her climb toward him. She hadn't covered a yard when the shot came.

Will-Joe saw her spin and fall, spilling down on her face in a river of rubble till a rock stopped her. She lay unmoving.

He twisted his head. Ulring stood atop the ridge, his grin a white smear in his hat shadow.

Deliberately, taking all the time in the world, he reloaded the Sharps. He never stopped grinning. Then his head tipped, his glance going above Will-Joe.

Miss Bethany was coming up the slope. Clutching her skirts in one hand, clutching them knee-high, stumbling, falling, getting up again, moving stubbornly upward toward the still form of the Navajo girl. She dropped on her knees and raised Rainbow Girl's head, then looked up toward Ulring.

He threw back his head and laughed.

'You beast! You filthy beast, Frank!'

She clawed up the Winchester, scrambled to her feet, and began to climb toward Will-Joe. Ulring started down the slope at an easy swinging stride. Clenching his jaws, Will-Joe shifted sideways till a leaning slab of rock cut him off from Ulring. Only brief cover. And it did not really matter. He would be dead in a minute. He heard Miss Bethany's soft hard-driven sobs as she toiled upward.

Ulring dropped into the pocket and looked at Will-Joe flattened against the slab ten yards away, just his face showing. Ulring tipped up the Sharps. A weapon, Will-Joe knew, that would tear a man open like wet paper.

'How you doing, boy?' Ulring said lazily. And fired.

Rock splinters exploded a foot from Will-Joe's face. Tearing pain in his flesh. He grabbed at his face with both hands; the crutch

241

skidded away and he fell. His ears roared with Ulring's laughter. He tried to blink his eyes clear ... a red fog stained them. Terror seized him. Then he realized he was only blinded by the blood streaming down from a wide shallow cut over his brows.

He carefully wiped his eyes clean with his bandanna. Suddenly Ulring was quiet. And cautiously, very slowly, Will-Joe crutched himself upright again.

Miss Bethany stood on the rim of the pocket. Shoulders heaving. Greenfire eyes fixed on Ulring.

'You best drop that, Beth.'

She looked down at the rifle in her hands. And brought it up level, awkwardly working the lever. Ulring tossed the Sharps from his right hand to his left, whipped up his Colt and fired in one smooth motion.

She screamed. Blood sprang across her torn sleeve. Her face was white with shock. She dropped the Winchester.

'Better,' Ulring smiled. 'I just broke the skin ... there's all kinds of time, sweetheart.'

'You're mad, Frank—'

Still smiling, Ulring sheathed his pistol and walked over to her. His hand lashed across her face. She fell, rolling on her side. She stared up at him, drawing a hand across her broken lips.

'You don't want to go talking like that, honey. I got a lot better in mind for us. Right after I settle things with breed boy.'

He picked up the Winchester and tossed it to the ground a few yards away, then wheeled and started toward the rock that hid Will-Joe.

'Come on out, boy. It's all up.'

Without moving his eyes, Will-Joe saw Miss Bethany lift up on her elbow. Her hand had slipped into her jacket pocket and it came out holding a small gun. She fired. Ulring jerked in mid-stride, grunting, turning then. He stared at the little single-shot pistol, then slowly raised his right arm, peering under the sleeve. A spreading circle of red dyed the armpit of his shirt.

'Well, I'm a son of a bitch,' he said, chuckling.

His pistol blurred up. Four shots slammed off, kicking up dirt around the prone woman. Dirt spewed in her face; a bullet ripped her skirt. Silence. A reeking swirl of powdersmoke. She lay on her side, face buried in her arms; soft jerking sobs wracked her body.

'You know, honey,' he drawled, 'I could get real upset with you.'

He walked to her, dropped the Sharps, grabbed a fistful of her jacket and yanked her up to her knees. His hand cracked across her face. It smashed her on the backswing, then struck again.

Will-Joe, already moving, let his good leg take his weight in a long lunging step, crutch leaping out to catch another straining step. Another. Two yards from Ulring's back he stopped, balanced on his good leg and hefted the crutch by its butt end.

Ulring grunted in the fury of a crunching blow on the woman's face. Then he let her drop and began to turn around just as Will-Joe swung the crutch in a short savage arc. The heavy forked end smashed Ulring across the face. The crutch cracked, splitting at the end. Ulring went down, rolling over in the rubble, hands to his face.

Will-Joe, his balance gone, dropped to the ground. Ulring had rolled across the barrel of his Sharps. The stock was inside Will-Joe's reach; he grabbed at it, but Ulring's weight pinned it solidly.

Will-Joe's glance flew to his Winchester where Ulring had thrown it. Some four yards away. He floundered toward it. Behind him, Ulring groaned, starting to move. Will-Joe clamped his hands on the Winchester and heaved up on one elbow.

Ulring was on his knees, the split skin of his forehead runneling blood; sand smeared it across half his face. He brought up his pistol, catching Will-Joe in line, and the trigger snapped. Empty chamber. Five shots.

He let the pistol drop, grabbing up the empty Sharps, lunging onto his feet, coming after Will-Joe as he swung the Sharps back by its barrel for a crushing blow.

No time for Will-Joe to shift his body around, much less take aim. He jammed the

Winchester's butt against a rock, setting it in a blind aim backwards, right hand steadying the barrel. He gauged blindly: raising the barrel—too high—tipping it down.

Ulring loomed like a tree; the sky seemed full of him. The sun behind his head aureoled his hair like a tawny nimbus, his face a dark broken mask, streaked and snarling, between his raised arms. Will-Joe's left hand jerked the trigger.

The shot slammed Ulring in the chest, stopping him as if he had run into a wall. Suddenly the blue-bright sky was empty, and he was down on his back. His clutching fist came up to his chest, then twitched open and was still.

Will-Joe did not get up quickly. His muscles hardly seemed to work. He picked up his crutch. The end had split off, but the rest of it would take his weight. He maneuvered delicately to his feet. He limped to the rim of the ledge, dreading to look down.

Rainbow Girl was moving. Crawling up the rocks with a terrible inching effort, using one arm only. She stopped and looked upward. The despair in her face gave way to something else.

'Jahzini . . .' Her voice was very faint.

A trembling seized him. He stood quietly till it ebbed to a few rubbery tremors.

Miss Bethany came shakily up beside him. Her face was bloody and bruised, but her back was straight, her eyes clear. He wondered what kind of country it was, that New England which had produced her. Granite country, it must be. Granite people.

'I think she is all right,' Miss Bethany said. 'The shock . . . the bullet passed through her arm. And her head hit when she fell.'

He started limping down the ridge.

'Will-Joe . . . let me help you.'

'You always help.' He stopped and looked up at her, and almost smiled. 'I help myself now, thank you.'

He moved on down the slope, tired and stumbling, catching himself somehow, going straight on down the ridge. All that he had been thinking, fragments of talk, scenes jostling against each other, memories jumbling, Dennis McAllister and Bloodgood and Ulring, even Miss Bethany—all of it was unfocusing now, letting go, blurring away as if it had never been.

Only Rainbow Girl was left. Only she was real.

We hope you have enjoyed this Large Print book. Other Chivers Press or G.K. Hall & Co. Large Print books are available at your library or directly from the publishers.

For more information about current and forthcoming titles, please call or write, without obligation, to:

Chivers Press Limited
Windsor Bridge Road
Bath BA2 3AX
England
Tel. (01225) 335336

OR

G.K. Hall & Co.
P.O. Box 159
Thorndike, Maine 04986
USA
Tel. (800) 223-2336

All our Large Print titles are designed for easy reading, and all our books are made to last.